P9-CDJ-840

WINGS OF STONE

for Gretchen and Frank ı .

WINGS OF STONE

Linda Ty-Casper

readers international

Copyright © Linda Ty-Casper and Readers International, Inc., 1986
First published by Readers International, Inc., New York and
London, whose editorial branch is at 8 Strathray Gardens, London
NW3 4NY, England. US/Canadian inquiries to Subscriber Service
Department, P.O. Box 959, Columbia, Louisiana 71418, USA.

All rights reserved in all languages

Cover painting by the Filipino artist Ben Cabrera

Design by Jan Brychta
Typesetting by Grassroots Typeset, London NW6
Printed and Bound in Great Britain by Richard Clay
(The Chaucer Press) Ltd., Bungay, Suffolk

ISBN 0-930523-26-1 Hardcover
ISBN 0-930523-27-X Paperback

Johnny Manalo pulled back the drapes on entering the hotel room. He had asked for a view facing Manila Bay, but at midnight all he could see from the sixth floor of the Silahis appeared to be dark shapes over water. He let the drapes fall. With the stiff weave roughing his hand, he turned to tip the bellboy, who was still carrying the suitcases, 24-inch gray Samsonites almost half as tall as he. At six feet, give or take an inch, Johnny Manalo felt like a foreigner beside him.

"Thank you, sir. Very much." The bellboy's face was one big smile. "Thank you."

That delighted Johnny. To turn on such gratitude at Manila International Airport, he had tipped five-dollar bills. What the hell. He had been away thirteen years; and if the First Lady tipped hundred-dollar bills in New York, Johnny Manalo could surely pass out five, even ten, in his own country. Besides, it was his money, not the taxpayers'.

Alone in the room, Johnny switched on two side lamps, then turned off the overhead bulbs encased in *capiz*. Immediately space was divided into overlapping circles of light. It reminded him of his landlady's garden in Watertown. As narrow and dark as a pool, its flowerbeds were like lilypads pierced by sunlight.

Johnny peeled off his jacket. The left cuff caught on the digital watch, going-away gift from the three friends he had notified of his trip. An hour before midnight. March 1st shifting fast into 2nd. Back in Boston it would be noon, still February 29, the day he flew out of Logan to Chicago's O'Hare on Northwest Orient Flight 28. Departure and arrival merged. How did one disengage from time which, coming to an end here, began again there?

Refusing to reflect upon this, Johnny Manalo looked about his room, standing beside the double bed covered with the same material as the drapes but in reversed reds, in the center of which unlikely shadows lay, the shapes of human bodies asleep together. He turned to face the opposite wall.

Above another lamp, daubs of black, white and red acrylic fixed two fighting cocks in mid-air collision. What at first he thought were branches turned out to be the arms of *aficionados*, reenacting the fury.

Intrigued, he sat on the bed to work at separating the roosters feather by feather, but was soon trying to account for the present moment. After twenty-one hours of flying, five or seven more spent waiting to board—losing count by refusing to adjust his watch to the various time zones—an hour and thirty minutes since landing at Manila, his excitement at being home after thirteen years in the States had turned into dread.

Eyes fixed on the fighting cocks, he saw only the outline of their combat as he flexed his shoulders and began half-heartedly to stretch. No reason he should not be asleep. Pulling off his shoes—he never laid them side by side in hotel rooms—he recalled that they had disembarked at the same gate as Ninoy Aquino.

"Is that the tarmac?" the Filipino from Chicago had asked the stewardess on the way through the passenger door. "Same exact tarmac down there?" The man finally answered himself by turning to Johnny Manalo, "If I had gone home last August, I might have taken the same flight. I could have become part of history."

Johnny walked over to the hotel window and cast another

glance toward Manila Bay. The same dark shapes rose and fell where he supposed it to be. History was only someone's memory, was never true. He had no ambitions to enter into it, took a sabbatical not to take part in it. Why had he come, then?

Unable to give himself an answer, he thought about the man who had wanted to see the land rising up to him as they landed, and had asked to change seats." "No sweat," Johnny had replied, though he wanted his window seat back as soon as they had switched.

Standing at the hotel window, peering out between the drapes, it began to matter that no one had seen him off at Logan Airport—it was a workday and he had wanted it that way; that no one met him here because he had let no one know he was coming. The man who had asked for his seat, who had slept through the two dinners and one breakfast served aboard, but once the descent began kept his face pressed to the window, had had two dozen sending him off at O'Hare, twice that many fighting to carry his boxes after he cleared Manila Customs.

But how could Johnny call his father to tell him he was coming when at any airport in between he might have turned back? He had taken the trip not to go anywhere, not even home—he had brought no homecoming presents, no *pasalubongs*—but simply to take off, to be free of the earth for the duration of the flight. Having touched down in Manila, he was ready to fly back on his open-ended return ticket.

From sitting up one full day at least, muscles tightly bunched with the effort of occupying only the space of his seat, Johnny Manalo felt sore all over. He had spent the entire trip with his eyes closed, waiting to arrive, refusing ear plugs for the movies and fending off all conversations from the Chicago Filipino, who was ready to recite his life story for the price of attention.

He walked back to the bed, did a couple of knee bends, side stretches, and then laid himself down. In Boston when he felt this wrecked, he would lie in bed waiting for rain to thunder on the roof, to fall until yards and streets were joined in a flood. That had happened only once in thirteen years. What he missed were the powerful rains of his childhood when plants and houses drowned, and grown trees were pulled up by the roots. Nature was gentler in Massachusetts. Now and then, however, a hurricane came inland, throwing twelve- or sixteen-foot high waves against the buildings along the shore, tumbling them together so coast guardsmen had to tie their craft to the top windows in order to rescue the occupants of soggy houses.

Johnny Manalo's thoughts returned to the way time mixed up boundaries, came and was still coming so that it was possible the present was already forever. Somewhere. His father was the one who worried over life's puzzles. After a patient of his died, his father tried to figure out how, despite all his medical efforts, life had managed to slip away. To Johnny it made no difference if there was life before death or only after.

I should have called him at the airport, Johnny thought, imagining his father's surprise. But suppose he had gone on? How long would his father wait, and where?

The phone rang once, then stopped; rang again, then silence.

Johnny Manalo leaped up from the bed, but could not move. He felt locked in by that awful sound. It had been only a year since early morning phone calls waked him with threats to tip off U.S. Immigration that he was an illegal alien—TNT—working on an expired student visa, dodging discovery by changing rooms as often as one changes sheets.

What was it now? Some technology unleashed by Immigration and programmed to track him down; or the *psi* component of matter that lingered long after its source

4

had disintegrated? Sound, for example, loose in the cosmos and travelling long after the voice that uttered it had died?

He listened and waited. Running and dodging, practised almost a lifetime, kept him on edge. That could be what immortality was all about: total fear and terror, total joy— life lived to the hilt, no holds barred. The entire deep truth, philosophers said, was that everything had its source in fear, in anxiety and doubt. If so, he was lucky. Those primal realities were his life-long confidants.

He could not block out the phone's ringing by telling himself it was in the next room, the other guy's worry. Was there another guy, or was he the only one on that floor? Tourists were supposed to have been scared off by the bombings in the early 80s. Then Ninoy was shot to kingdom-come right in view of the airport TV cameras that happened—just happened not to be working.

As usual his thoughts were ranging far afield. It came from misusing his life. Adrift in the States, he had had no sense of purpose or connection. He might have been expelled from an atrophied womb. There were things he could not understand or explain, like the suddenness of his decision to come home.

Glancing by chance at the mirror, he laughed at himself. Who, seeing him in Dior shirt and Ralph Lauren slacks, would guess he had these doubts rotting inside? Those philosophers, claiming it was human to rest in doubt, were merely trying to outwit one another with gibberish.

The air conditioner was laboring as hard as a boat's motor. Johnny Manalo recalled that 1984 was the year, Orwell's year, when he planned to buy a boat and live anchored in Boston Harbor, or at the marina in Charlestown. Close to the *SS Constitution*, he could watch the wooden hull being turned around each year so it would weather on both sides. Either place, he would be within walking distance of the MBTA. He liked the anonymity of the subways, the slow-motion rush. As soon as he got back, he would go to the Boston Boat Show and pick out his baby. The way he had been moving up to bigger cars with more options, he would move up to larger boats until, on weekends, he could race out to Long Island. No longer limited to Nantucket and Martha's Vineyard, he would become ocean-going, free of the earth.

What about Rose Quarter? He could leave behind the attic apartment with shutters he had stained to match the ceiling-high bookshelves. But what about the second floor apartment which he entered from the backstairs, so that he had never seen himself coming into the boxlike foyer with its ornate wall mirror—the only new object in her place besides the bed? What about Rose Quarter?

Johnny Manalo walked over to take another look at the Bay. But before he reached the window he stopped to switch his watch back to Eastern Standard Time. Something fixed, in case he ran into surprises. Then he returned to the bed and lay down.

It was too late to phone his father. There had been no time to write either. This would not have made a difference, except that he had made no call from overseas. He had forgotten, having assumed as usual that whatever crossed his mind passed on into the thoughts of whoever else was involved.

Once the idea of coming home had occurred to him, it took only two days to take off: to call for the tickets and pick them up, to pass by the BayBank at Harvard Square for travellers checks, to invite three friends for a farewell *despedida*, then take Rose Quarter for a dinner of curried mussels at the new deli on Mass Ave, where he announced that he would be back April 1st. "That's April Fools' Day," she had remarked, pulling her brioche apart. The ordinariness of the place—her choice—seemed inappropriate to going off on an adventure into eternity.

He could have called his father from O'Hare, or from Manila airport upon landing, or from the hotel after checking in. In the morning I'll call Papá, Johnny Manalo decided. His father would be asleep. Bedtime came early for those over 80. To arrive at his father's age, all he had to do was add forty-three to his own. Easy calculation. What was difficult to figure out was why his father had waited so long to have him.

Trying to sleep was worse than fighting air turbulence. Refusing to count sheep (Rose Quarter counted geese, Canadian geese landing web-clawed on the Charles River) he reconsidered the sudden turns of the mind by which he had finally come back. Occasionally in thirteen years he had considered the possiblity of coming home; with much guilt when he recalled all the letters he did not write, with grave impatience when the Boston winter made him hurl himself bodily against the walls to get his blood going again. Determined not to endure another snowstorm, cursing all the way to his classes or to the hospital where he calibrated X-rays—a patient burns and they know Johnny Manalo has slipped up—he devised reasons not to go home, against reasons to go.

What about Rose Quarter? Right away she opened the door the first time he ever knocked. Not at all surprised, as if she had been standing there since the beginning of time, waiting. "Would you like a cup of fresh-brewed coffee?" He would. Several cups—black. Each time she offered to pour, he accepted the brew, which then kept him awake until just before the sun came up over the oak in the morning sky, surprising him in bed with her.

He had never been able to explain why he had knocked at her kitchen door when he was on his way to browse at the sale tables of Harvard Bookstore, then to order a sundae at Bailey's. It must have been another blind chance, a random coincidence redirecting his entire life.

Always, on the point of a solution, he would act out of desperation, opt for a temporary reprieve that only locked him into another problem. That was the irrationality he wanted to be rid of, that must have been bred in him by defective genes. What else could explain why, having dodged Immigration for eight years after his doctorate, he married Rose Quarter for a Green Card when there was a bill pending in Congress that would give illegal aliens the right to residence!

Married Rose Quarter for the alien registration card? The idea, of course, did not enter his mind that way. If it had, he might have saved himself years of hiding, the measly jobs, those fearswept years that had battered him down like a built-in hurricane. Johnny Manalo shipwrecked inside his own body. He was in her kitchen, a cup of brewed coffee in his hand, a long silence between him and Rose Quarter, when casually he said a friend had just paid three thousand dollars to marry a woman who agreed to divorce him after he acquired permanent residence. "No kidding," Rose said. "I'll marry you, Johnny, and you needn't pay me a cent. Just for old times sake. We'll have a friendly divorce after your card arrives. Mary need not know."

Mary Brewer owned the house, living in the first floor apartment. In the course of their friendship, Johnny learned that Rose had been brought there as a foster child. Mary liked to recall her husband having awnings installed and the custom wallpaper he designed put up all over the house. Rose Quarter remembered that Mary's husband had reneged on his promise to adopt her. After he died Rose was on her own and able to pay for the rooms on the second floor. "Mary mentioned adoption then, but I didn't encourage it. Yet she's the only mother I ever had."

The two women had supper together regularly, went to the Episcopal church on Sundays and, in the middle of summer, took one long trip to Bar Harbor, Maine. Once he brought both of them on a foliage trip over the Mohawk Trail up to the New York border. Mary had said, "Wouldn't it be nice if we could drive on to Niagara Falls?" He would have kept on, except the next day was Monday. That was one thing Johnny still regretted not being able to do for them.

He could have saved himself from guilt if he had only waited for the Simpson-Mazzoli Bill to pass. By the time he returned it could be law, entitling him to a Green Card on his own. Owing Rose Quarter nothing. Yet what exactly *did* he owe her?

As if he might find the answer etched there, Johnny faced the wall of the fighting cocks. This time, blurred by weariness, his eyes saw suns in collision, matter smashed by machines built miles long to recreate the first explosion that astrophysicists claimed had created life and assembled the Universe.

In succession two images unrelated to his thoughts escaped from memory. One was the light shimmering over Winthrop and George's Island—summer picnic ground for the Filipino Association of Greater Boston—as Northwest Orient Flight 28 lifted, then winged back over the land toward the west. The other was the sun cutting across ricefields, fishponds, and Manila Bay as the Philippine Airlines jet lifted up from the old Manila airport that morning of August 21, 1971—his first flight ever. So stunning was this parting sight that he had been unprepared for the news waiting at San Francisco. Two fragmentation grenades—U.S. Vietnam War issue—had exploded at an opposition rally at Plaza Miranda. Nine killed and a hundred wounded—including every Liberal candidate present. It happened the evening of the day he left, by West Coast time the evening he arrived. Time overlapping again.

The two images, one fresh, the other deep in memory, joined far segments of his life the way the murmur of the air conditioner pulled the long room together. Where else was it today here, tomorrow there?

Johnny sat up to clear his thoughts of the puzzle, began undressing but finally could not unbutton his shirt in the hotel room that reminded him of Rose Quarter's bed. Only awkwardly, and always as if for the first time, did he take off his clothes with her watching.... She was incredibly white, part of the white sheets she let out by pulley from her kitchen window to air-dry on the line. The overhead light fixtures made her walls, papered in white, appear to be a drinking glass being emptied, bottoms up, with the last sticky drops sliding heavily toward his open mouth. Waiting for her to come, he imagined someone looking down on them and mistaking Rose Quarter for a fish—not a mermaid, but a soft spongy fish resting on the absolute bottom of the ocean, very white and tinged with pink where he had pressed upon her....

Suppose he called her up. "It's two o'clock Friday morning here. What time is it there?"

It was no use. He must stop thinking back. Here and now were what mattered.

He began taking out the contents of his pockets: keys, tabs, quarters and a dime, Clorets, pens with supermarket logos, nail-clipper, the Swiss penknife that had everything from scissors to tweezers and toothpick. Strange charms, he thought, sorting them by size and piling them neatly on the bedside table. The sight of those random objects unsettled him. He felt improperly summed up by them.

All his life he had been waiting to come into a strong emotion that would bind all moments past with those to come, but what he remembered was bafflement and regret; and rage from failure, from the knowledge of certain and continuing failure. He and Rose Quarter felt things differently in their bodies, yet love with the sure intensity of fire was supposed to weld together not only bodies but, thereafter, thoughts and will and soul, those unwieldy and often unreal attributes of self.

Love was supposed to be like singing for the first time, each time.

He was bitter that he would bind himself in so simple, so commonplace a desire when serial relationships, neither sequential nor lasting, were the "in thing", the *macho* way—life lived at a rush, escaping from someone into another. Like a fool, he wanted a relationship so close it was not possible to give the other a name other than his. Urgencies only ended up in departures.

It was high time he became practical. Like Steve Paz, who had renovated three old mansions in the South End into $800-a-month apartments and with the proceeds had bought a house in Weston worth half a million. While all Johnny's energy went into fantasizing about love that no longer existed. Prehistoric. Even the first time was no fragile singing, no first-time trembling. This was the age of corporate messiahs, of shuttles to the moon, of *in vitro* conceptions; and what he wanted was still Maria Clara! That was from some medieval monastery, that crazy desire. Human generations don't co-exist the way time does.

It could not be that fragile trembling with Rose Quarter, ever. Out of *delicadeza*, the desire not to offend, he had not been able to bring up the friendly divorce she had promised, could only wait for her to suggest it the way she had proposed the fake marriage. He had given her the opportunity by inviting her to dinner at Copley Plaza. "To celebrate my Green Card," he said to her. But she could not be tempted any more than calculated. After he got back to Boston, he would give her another chance. Dinner at the Westin. And if that did not work, a lawyer could prepare the papers while he disappeared. Suppose he simply did not go back?

Shirttail out, Johnny Manalo dropped back on the bed,

though he was not sleepy. Still on Boston time, thirteen hours behind Manila, he was wide awake. Soon he was sweating as if he were lying on a ripped waterbed, narrow shallows, summer waves off Florida. Something had stopped. The lights were out. The air conditioner quiet. He thought of buzzing the desk clerk but decided to check for himself, to see if his room had an outside door. In a late, late movie a man found himself sealed inside his hotel room, the door papered over. Johnny sensed a parallel with the time overlap, which shifted boundaries.

Emergency lights were on in the hall. A bellboy, not the one he had tipped, went by. "Temporary, sir. Aircons will go on right away, sir. Anything I can do for you, sir?"

Back in the room Johnny could not recall anything of that encounter. Was there really a bellboy or had he imagined it? Sleep-starved but unable to sleep with his internal clock all wound up, he must have hallucinated.

Sleep was impossible in the darkness. Dark rooms reminded him of disconnected phones, of being afraid to stop seeing Rose Quarter for fear she might turn him in. She still could. Anonymous tip. But there was the marriage. She would implicate herself.

There was no reason not to fall asleep, Johnny thought. Jet lag was just another excuse. The daily body rhythm was subject to the will, and dislocations were inevitable only for those afraid to be surprised in their sleep. With that Green Card, actually white, what was there to worry him? He was a registered alien....

But it was fake, his conscience outfaced him: outright fake based on a phony marriage. He, Johnny F. Manalo, had undermined the system by importing corruption. Intending to liberate himself in the United States, he had fouled it instead for himself and for everyone who lived there. No way now would it be the same land of the free, even if no one discovered the hairline crack. It's the exact same thing, he accused himself, as inserting defective microchips into a multimillion-dollar defense program, or selling secrets to the KGB.

He fell asleep. And dreamed. He was chasing a thief who had made off with his alien registration card. As hooked tails began sprouting out of his arms, the thief threw out boxfuls of Green Cards that glued themselves to Johnny's body like scales and turned him into a mangy tree. On each card, all his, was the soft white face of Rose Quarter. Listen, he called out and woke up shouting: It is mine, mine....

Mine: Juan F. Manalo, age 38, permanent resident, port of entry Honolulu, August 21, 1971. He could not stop the chase: slipping, falling and rushing....1791 port of entry permanent August Johnny, Johnny 38....

Out of breath from running, he fumbled the temporary terms of immortality.

"I just arrived. Just now this morning. Noon...." Johnny Manalo's words jostled each other at the gate of his father's house. His voice dropped as the words turned into outright lies meant to absolve, but instead, indicting him. "I took a taxi. To save you the trouble of having to pick me up."

Whether out of surprise or disbelief, or from straining to absorb the disparate explanations, his father said nothing. Johnny began to feel like a large, hastily made-up body standing without shadows under the bougainvilleas that climbed over the gate and lifted up the fence with thornclad branches, matted with leaf and flower. Confounded by the lies he had not intended to say but which, once uttered, impeded fact and truth, Johnny gave up. Silently, he brought his father's hand to his forehead.

When his father stepped back, a half-stagger that tapped Johnny's fears, he thought for a moment that he had not been recognized. Looking up at the sign below the upstairs window—Magtanggol B. Manalo, *Medico Cirujano*—under which his father squarely stood, Johnny Manalo wondered how he might introduce himself without having to give his name.

After a silence that seemed hours in passing, his father took another step closer to the house, giving him room to enter. "Come in."

And though only those words were said, words that could have been used with a peddler or a bill collector, Johnny felt relieved. He imposed a feeling upon them, an urgency which he then interpreted as his father's happiness on seeing him. Whether it was or not, the rough and ill-proportions of Johnny's fears disappeared. Confidence took their place. He felt capable of making everything right again. From a course on self-esteem Johnny Manalo had learned that no matter how little reason there is for confidence, one has to act boldly. Timidity invites rejection, results in isolation.

"So we still have the pool," Johnny put his lessons quickly into practice. He remembered his father had filled the pool with *tilapia* just after the species had been introduced from Africa. Reproducing, they quickly outstripped the pool's resources, and it was now a lilypond again. Its stillness gave Johnny the feeling of his having been awaited, there in that garden where nothing stirred the shadows of the leaves. The yellow center of the floating lily reflected the petals of *champacas* flowering in a corner on leafless branches.

"Does Martin know you're here?"

"No, Papá. I came to you first," Johnny answered, pleased to be able to declare truthfully that his father came first, though it was because he had forgotten Martin, or more precisely, had lost the habit of thinking about his brother. Martin, he remembered, never failed to declare his concern for their mother and their father. It was always, "I couldn't go without seeing you first," or, "I think of you even when

I am at a reception." It had to be insincere, since once Martin had left home he returned only on holidays and briefly.

At the same time he and his father looked up at the house that still bore some reddish paint. Yellow bordered, it resembled the old houses in the French Quarter of New Orleans. Up the window grilles climbed vines of morning glory. The blue flowers were like bits of sky swollen against the windows.

"Nothing has changed," Johnny said, amazed and perplexed, for there was something definitely unfamiliar about the house. It was not only that the tree in front had grown past the roof and was ranging wide, its crown connecting the house to the neighbor's roof and trees.

"Martin used to swing from that tree." His father followed Johnny's gaze. The stoop of his shoulders gave the impression of someone's hand upon them.

Didn't he, too, swing from the same tree and, once, try to build a treehouse? Then, sure of the answer but not of the feeling of exclusion, Johnny thought about Rose Quarter, imagined her skinny-dipping in the pool, white and soft as an early morning sky or the ocean frothing with white caps. Wary of his feelings in his father's house, Johnny tried to shake off all thoughts of Rose Quarter before he uttered them; but like a prism full of endless repetitions, she hung stubbornly in his mind, forcing his other thoughts to bend to her absent body.

A soft-stemmed flower of the gingerplant leaned against the stucco. "*Camia*," he named it, staking a claim to his father and the house, to the times when he outfought Martin in that garden over who would bring the flowers up to their mother.

"Let's go in," his father said. "You must be tired."

Once the door was closed after them, Johnny felt like a first-time visitor required to work his way into the affection and esteem of the household, when what he wanted was to run all through the house, to look for things he remembered, to rediscover what he had forgotten. Instead of heading for his room, he waited to be told: Go ahead. Do what you want. It's your house.

Old issues of *National Geographic, Photography* and *Readers Digest* were in separate piles in the receiving room. Pushing a chair into line, turning on the ceiling fan and bringing up an ashtray, his father allowed Johnny to stand by himself at the window, looking out.

Only parts of the other houses could be seen, in patches as irregular as the shadow of the leaves. *Campanillas* wove their vines into the steel landing strips which formed the common part of the fence. Full of moisture, the sky was clear but heavy, reminding Johnny of a recurrent dream of walking across a field of strange trees sprouting. When he tried to touch them, his hand brushed against lime stalactites, dripping, cagelike—he was walking inside his skull.

"As soon as the convention is over, I'll move in," Johnny Manalo said, announcing his intention but unable to drop the initial lie. He waited for his father to detect it, to lead him out of it by challenging him. When none came, Johnny went on, "I had no firm plan to attend or I would have written, or called. Just this Monday when I woke up, I had no idea...." He glanced at his watch. It indicated Friday, March 2: 12 noon. Rose Quarter would be turning on the 11 o'clock late, late Thursday news on Channel Four and, promptly, falling asleep.

"Beer?" his father asked, standing beside the sofa whose every cushion sagged from the weight of all the patients squeezed against each other, waiting. They sat on the steps, stood against the doorway....

"San Miguel?" Johnny replied with another question, going on to say that when on a tour with Fel, the time his friend worked as a travel agent, he had seen signs for San Miguel all over Spain.

"Would you prefer coffee?"

"Whatever you'll have, Papá." He was not used to being served by his father in that house. Always it was his mother reminding Salud, "The doctor might be hungry. Bring something to the clinic. A glass of milk. Chocolate." Always what would please his father was served at the table; so fish, because the doctor disliked red meat. Meals were at his convenience, too; when he was through with his patients. "I don't care," Johnny almost added. In time he realized this would sound ungrateful. *Ingrato* his father called people he disliked; *ingrato* covering every kind of vice, omission and malice; not just ingratitude. "Whatever is easy, Papá."

"Neither requires effort," his father answered.

Not knowing what had been decided by that reply, Johnny felt compelled to cover the moment. He took out his wallet and pulled out his Green Card. "They want ears showing," he explained the side view. "And yes, it's white really, not green." Then somehow, he returned to the lie that wanted to be pushed down his throat: "I would have called but the lines were busy...." He wanted to be challenged, to be wrestled back to the truth knowing he might make up another lie alternating with this unless he was completely purged.

His father handed back the card, then proceeded up the stairs that ran alongside one wall.

Johnny watched him clinging to the bannister. The last time he was in that house, his father was going down those steps at a run, black bag in one hand, the newspaper in the other, on the way to the hospital. It was a fearsome thing to see his father old in that house. So Johnny Manalo started talking, freely associating with objects in the room, a shell, the *zapote* outside with fruits resembling apples, bells, bringing out in words the contents of the heart that could not let go of memory.

He was afraid again, someone who inhabited another's

17

body, about to be pushed out by the bursting of circles that freed what preferred to be enclosed; full of many fears, even of that self-preserving distance with his father now that he was home. Following his father up the stairs, he willed back Rose Quarter into his thoughts but knew she would not help him. He could not go up without being asked. He turned on the stairs and walked down.

From where he stood, he continued to talk. Having had an hour's sleep at the most out of four or five spent trying, he was using far too many words to explain what was clear enough. But he needed words, the encumbrance of sound to fill the space lengthening between himself and his father. The words were like so many dead balls in a tournament. He wanted someone to tell him to shut up. There was nothing to say, though everything to explain.

Light coming in through the window tempted him to speak. It had pulled him out of his hotel bed with its unbearable brightness over the water. Dressing quickly, he had followed it into Dewey Boulevard, now Roxas. Casually, as if he had lived his life in five-star hotels, he took the newspaper a boy held out to him, paid a dollar but did not look at the news, merely rolled it up to have something to hold. Soon enough he discovered he could not have seen the waves from his hotel window even if he had come during the daylight. His window faced Malate Church across the plaza, having only an oblique view of the Bay. This had been reclaimed for the Cultural Center, the complex of hotel, convention and film festival sites. THe waterfront was now out where the breakwaters used to be. Having intended to walk the length of seawall he remembered, Johnny was so upset by the change that he hailed a taxi and gave directions to his father's house.

Standing there, waiting for his father to speak—why was it that everything lay in waiting?—he continued to feel the loss of boundaries, so that he watched the light coming onto the floor as if he might never see it that way again.

An old fantasy of his had been to save his Stateside earnings and buy along the old boulevard so he could watch the sun set on Manila Bay, see the waves rushing in on the tides to leave shells outside his door. Part of these thoughts, which occasionally entered his sleep, went on towards the Pasay out to where outriggered boats tossed spray towards the yachts, their prows heading away from the large tomblike structures he did not recognize.

He heard his father open-closing doors upstairs and recalled that his own room was downstairs, beside the clinic. He walked toward it but was distracted by the bust of the Sacred Heart of Jesus enclosed in glass *viriña* above the piano. Patients on entering sometimes genuflected before it. There was another piano on the upper floor. A chromo of Saint Cecilia hung above it. When she still played the piano, he imagined his mother fixing her gaze upon it while her fingers ran over the keys.

Unaccompanied by much feeling, he recalled all this while he studied the green lines on the tile floor that reproduced the pattern on the cane chairs. The house looked worn down by all the patients who waited for their turn in the clinic.

After some time his father came down, bringing a box that required both hands to hold. As if bidding Johnny to enter for the first time, his father stopped at the bottom of the stairs and said, "I had dreamed of your coming just like this, without suitcases."

Johnny Manalo's father laid the box on the coffee table before sitting down across from where Johnny waited. They did not speak. The narrow space between them might as well have been a map of where they should not cross.

Johnny felt they had sat that way before, had already lived

19

through that moment; possibly because his memory of his father was chiefly of a man with fierce passions, unwavering in the face of reasonable appeals. And now his father looked as if everything he wanted to say had been said and there was no one, any more, that he wanted to meet: someone, as painlessly as possible, using up what was left to him of mortal time.

This observation led Johnny to recall the woman on Boston Common shouting, "All you holy people, come and follow me." Large, in winter clothes of several layers in the middle of summer, the woman looked to her left, then to her right without turning her head, her eyeballs in a fixed arc like that of a blind person's cane switching back and forth to make sure the way ahead was clear.

Unable to stand the silence, Johnny walked to the door and out into the garden. In clay pots leading to the gate he recognized *malvarosa*, whose spicy stinging leaves his mother liked to crush inside her pillows. White and red with a design of trellises, these were the same pots Salud tended while his mother would give commands from the doorway. All the while, his father would be locked in the clinic with his patients, bent over them, checking their pulses, examining their lungs or hearts but never looking directly into their eyes while he probed. Most of the patients came from the provinces, were at the gate before the sun came up, so they must have traveled at night.

His father took time from his ministrations only to attend annual medical banquets and conferences or to stand as sponsor at a wedding, a godfather at baptism or confirmation. Almost every child born in that clinic was his godchild.

Long ago, in rebellion against his father's odd parceling-out of his life, Johnny Manalo had decided his own would burst with daily excitement. But like his father's, his life had become a routine, circumscribed by what he did not have the energy to do. Only in fantasy did he soar.

In the garden he began to feel drowsy, so out of control of himself that he could no longer wonder what time it was in Boston. To keep awake he walked deeper into the garden. New bushes he could not name were now assembled beside paths of stones worn smooth by waves. He thought of the Lexington Gardens in North Hancock Street. There, in winter, tropical plants threw out blossoms you could not otherwise see without hiking halfway across the world.

Another lily opened in the pool.

Still, his father had not followed him out into the garden where, he imagined, the roots traced underground the shape of the branches above. He felt an ache standing there, as if things had ended; he missed being made to conform to the desire of another.

Between the lilypads he could see the opening sky. An insect dropped, disturbed the water. He wanted to shout, to be lifted out of that place, returned.... It must be jet lag distorting his senses, and he reacted by thinking he was merely another surface there, a foreign element being made to fit the landscape.

Hands in his pockets, fighting for control, he entered the house again, his steps jaunty to cover up the fact that he felt nausea, felt he was moving in a fog.

Just as he was about to speak, it occurred to Johnny that neither he nor his brother Martin had been given his father's first name: Magtanggol, Jr. He returned to his chair, unnerved by this thought. At least Martin could have named one of his sons Magtanggol III. One who protects, defends.

His father seemed not to have realized Johnny had gone out. Two cups of coffee, both untouched, were on the low dividing table. On reentering, Johnny smelled the damp old wood of the house and thought of decayed inheritance and children born to other people.

The sky blinked, or the light did through the window. His father got up to walk into the clinic with the box.

Watching, Johnny felt his father was moving about in another house, in several houses at once, his movements coming together in distant space the size of the circle formed by the thumb and forefinger.

Overpowering sleepiness was short-circuiting his senses. He tried to brace himself up with things that had been told him: Rose Quarter's father—or perhaps stepfather or even foster father, it was not clear in her narrations—was a postman who bought secondhand cars as an investment. Mary Brewer's husband owned a haberdashery on Atlantic Avenue near the piers. Only on his death did Mary discover he owned property scattered about Boston—triple-deckers in Dorchester and Charlestown—and only because the city liquidated them for nonpayment of taxes. He saved twine and shopping coupons, had the first television set in their block.

Curtains fluttered, allowing Johnny to glimpse the morning glory climbing up the grilles, each flower dark against the sky like an eye peeping. Johnny pulled himself up, stirred sugar into his cup but did not drink. The Sacred Heart was looking dead-eye at him. Was it placed there to calm patients down? And the St. Cecilia upstairs, because she was his mother's namesake? Suppose they had been switched?

It was not the way he had imagined coming home would be.

His father came out to sit across from Johnny. The box was no longer in his hand. Sitting forward, he stirred his cup, placed the teaspoon on the dish, his movements precise, clockwise and circling.

Tell me a secret, Johnny begged his father in his thoughts. Tell me anything to keep me awake, even something that deforms: lust or failure.... Falling asleep, Johnny pulled himself up by thinking of that Christmas when Mary Brewer, sipping eggnog in front of her fireplace, said out of the blue, "You young people have everything. Know everything.

When I was married, I knew nothing. And not much more afterward. Friends kept asking me to tell them how it was. I said, 'Get married and find out for yourselves.' I could not tell them, how could I say that it was like pushing marsh-mallows into a piggybank?''

Tell me..., he looked away from his father watching him. Tell me how you loved me into life. In what bed, what room, what hour of the day...?

His father nodded toward the one bedroom downstairs. "Lie down and rest. You look sleepy. Then we'll have lunch. And talk."

A heavy odor came at Johnny as he entered his room. He walked past it to the bed, narrower than he remembered, dropped down and stayed there though his falling into bed seemed to have released more of the odor and made it stronger, the way dropping onto old couches in rented rooms releases dust and the wings of dead moths.

Something of the power of language gone wild beat inside Johnny Manalo's sleep, making him toss, gagging him. In that sleep he was dashing off to the causeway around Dalahican and heading straight to the port of Cavite. At the bridge, once a year, he and his father used to buy a bushel of oysters to bring back to his mother. Then Rose Quarter entered the dream: out of a jar she was eating raspberry jam with a spoon. The color red stopped his lungs.

Fighting for breath he sat upright but, exhausted by the effort, fell asleep once more; saw himself, this time, claw-ing his way into a locked room, a little boy again, listening at night to the sounds going on inside the clinic where his father, stethoscope plugging his ears, could not hear his cry; was assigning patients—babies, grandathers, mothers, men in their prime—to their turn on the narrow metal bed, to their turn as the body lying there. Vases without flowers stood about in the garden under his mother's smile, and overturned drainpipes bred larvae.

In his dream, looking down through his father's eyes into the body prostrate on the bed, Johnny Manalo heard again the sound of lives that had waited to come to his father until they could no longer be saved; waited to come with cousins and townmates, mothers and children whose memories would forever hold those hours of waiting, the screams and the wailings, the faintings; the hope for healing which occasionally took place after medication had failed, the surprise of its coming easing the sad persistence of death in their minds.

Then the fragrance of *malvarosa* took over, along with the orchids blooming on long spikes under the trellises and exotic banana-like plants waving pink roses. Like some one waking up from divided dreams he could not carry away the picture of any one he had seen.

A boy coughed. A boy in blue rubber thongs sitting across the room from his bed. "They're having supper. They're waiting. I'm supposed to wake you up."

Johnny tried to rise but his strength could not hold him. A comforting ache spread over his body, pulling him back to sleep. Beside him he could feel Rose Quarter's cheek as soft as cream pie. He could feel her inward smile that did not move her lips. Why didn't she? he wondered, forgetting immediately what his question was about.

More than the fatness of her arms, the warmth of her hips pressed against his body, making him rise; her deep mouth, which he hated even while he was held by its warmth; what Johnny missed was the unsaid hostility between them. The struggle that was all his. He longed to taste, to see, to hear through another.

The boy coughed again.

Johnny sat up. How had the boy gotten inside his room? Then he saw the open door. Hadn't he pulled it shut the way he always did in Boston?

The boy said something about supper.

Supper? What day was it? Where was he in time? His ears were knocking like trapped air moaning through radiator pipes.

"Is he coming?" someone called from upstairs.

"Let him sleep," another answered.

He could not get up anyway. With hands seeking familiar holds on Rose Quarter's body, he burrowed under the pillows. Soon a dog's howling entered his dream, or came out of it.

Johnny Manalo had just checked his watch (he never took it off at night)—March 3, Saturday. The door was pushed wide open.

"Alejandro Martín!" His brother's full name came out of Johnny without hesitation, as if it were a volley prepared and aimed at the door, waiting for Martin to enter.

"Juaniyo! Papá and I took turns waking you up last night but you were either dead or pretending to sleep. Salud always said it's impossible to wake up someone who is not asleep. Get up. Let's go." Martin planted himself at the foot of the bed. "I'm taking you around before you disappear again. You never told me you were leaving for the States. You just left. In and out of the country as if you were just going to the corner."

They held each other off by the arms, mock fighting, pulling punches. Johnny recalled that when he left, Martin had been out of the country, somewhere in Europe with a girl. He would have brought this up, except that it was too early to counter Martin's accusations with his own.

"No middle-age paunch?" Martin stood away, looking at Johnny. "Anyway, let's go. I'll take you to my clubs. I'm due at the Makati Business Club. Only top executives. But

I don't suppose you'd like to discuss agriculture as against short-circuit industrialization. There's the breakfast club. How about racketball or squash? Tennis? Your choice."

"Where's Papá?"

"He was gone when I arrived. Perhaps he has taken a new devotion, making a round of the churches. We'll take the opposite pilgrimage...."

"I'll shower quickly." Johnny beat his way to the bathroom as if Martin were also headed there. He could not tell if his brother' dignity issued from the white *barong* with slashed cuffs, the black leather shoes or the brass belt buckle with leather inlay: AMM. Full of envy, he came out dripping, before he was ready to face his brother again.

"Mamá had your clothes washed and delivered to Don Bosco." Martin intercepted him on the way to the wardrobe. "She saved only the special-occasion ones. Nothing remains in fashion anyway. We can swing by the house. You might be able to wear mine. Or we could pass by your hotel... why a hotel? Papá is hurt, you know. He said you came without suitcases. At least three times he said that last night. I told him you wanted to be close to your convention. That's the reason you came, isn't it?"

"Of course," Johnny replied, hardly able to keep up with Martin's thoughts because he was still wondering why *his* clothes when it was Martin who had been born in the clinic. Actually, Salud said only that one night a woman gave birth in the clinic. "By morning she was gone. She had the most beautiful and innocent face.... She could have played the Virgin in the *sinakulo*. She never returned. The doctor got married and still she did not return. As if what she left behind were only her clothes."

The questions in Johnny's mind could no longer be answered, for Salud had died. In one of the few letters his father wrote, he informed Johnny, "The woman who took care of you and Martin died last Friday. I had masses said for her and buried her next to my wife." It was a formal letter that closed off further response. Each person was properly in his place: named, specified, the matter concerning them brought up and neatly concluded; all emotions spared. Which of them was that child?

"Don't bother making the bed. Time is running."

"I'll just throw the cover up."

"Anything special you want to do or see? It's Saturday. I can give you the whole day." A diamond ring took the place of the wedding band on Martin's finger. It caught the sunlight coming in through the window and threw a shower of light on the wall.

"Mamá's grave," Johnny answered, pulling the door shut. "I want to bring her flowers." On the way to the front door, he looked up the stairs and bolted up as if to take his leave of someone waiting there. Quickly he scanned the walls, the top of the piano, the Saint Cecilia, the tables. There was no picture of his mother. He tried the door to her room. It was locked.

The small boy was sitting at the dining table in the hall, dangling blue rubber thongs on his toes.

Johnny Manalo gave the boy an "AOK" signal before running down the stairs. It was meant for himself actually. He needed assurance that people could carry each other's pictures in their hearts.

Lacking urgency, their conversation was filled with simple civilities. It occurred to Johnny that he and his brother had never slept together. Martin's bedroom was beside their mother's upstairs because he had asthma and had to be tended at night by Salud, who had to be near their mother too, in case she called. The explanation once sufficed to take the edge off Johnny's envy.

On the way to the cemetery, Martin drove with one hand

while pointing out new places with the other. The strands of *sampaguita* flowers they had bought from a street vendor stuck to Johnny's fingers.

With effort, Johnny lifted the flowers above the weeds that overgrew the tombs. He looked down, not caring to see more than he had to. He could not recall ever being there as a child. No one had died while he was growing up. What family plots they had must have been in the province, too far a journey on All Saints' Day.

"Papá would not listen," Martin said, walking on to lead the way. "I wanted Mamá buried in Loyola, but he insisted here. You can't buy plots here in Malabon, and look how tall the grass is. Thick and tall enough to hide NPA guerillas." Martin stepped carefully between the stones. "And odors fit for an outhouse. Squatters are all over. You remember the slopes down to the fishponds? Squatters spring up like mushrooms there. Right on top of the garbage. It embarrasses the government. They are trucked to the provinces but they sneak back."

Johnny followed Martin past the mausoleums. Beyond the walls, the church looked like a ruined fortress.

"*Halá!*" Martin shouted at some children who had begun following them. Half-dressed, they moved easily among the tombs. Large white teeth appeared like cracks on their hard thin faces. "Go! Go before I call the priest."

Johnny stopped to look back at the children. "What harm is there?"

"I just don't want them anywhere close. You can't light a candle without their stealing it as soon as you turn around. They're up to no good. They might be pulling the car apart. Hurry. There's the place. That's it there."

Two whitewashed tombs side by side shared a cross of concrete, and a stone angel. Johnny checked the names to make sure, before he knelt, that he had found his mother's grave. He crossed himself. Then finding the flowers still in his hand, he got up to place them just below her name. The sun was hot.

Then he returned to where he had knelt and focusing on the tip of th angel's pointing finger began to pray. Martin scraping his shoes interrupted his thoughts. Worse than ragweed, pollen from the wild sunflowers blocked his sinuses. He had imagined an awning of soft vines over her resting place, pink and white *cadena de amor*—on Mother's Day he always felt sorry for classmates who wore white *cadena de amor* on their lapels to indicate their mothers were already dead.

"Tell Papá to move the bones now, while you're here," Martin remained standing. "I had an architect design a stone canopy for Loyola. I don't care if Salud is moved also. Reason with him. He says that place floods. Well, this place will be swept out to sea during one of the typhoons, and the caskets will have to be chained to the trees. Talk to Papá while you're here. He might listen to you. Are you ready? Let's go."

Johnny leaned over the flowers to take a few strands for Salud before whose tomb he did not kneel but only stood silent for a minute. The sun skimmed the porous surfaces of stone until each tomb, whitewashed, appeared to tear apart the sky.

"I hope you don't plan to go inside the church to light candles. It's getting late," Martin juggled his car key.

Johnny had not intended to, but now that Martin suggested otherwise, he bought some candles from the woman at the door and did not take the change she extended to him.

"Let her light the candles for you," Martin said, following Johnny past the wooden doors. "You've prayed outside."

"I want to go in." Johnny stood beside the large stone angel holding a shell where the holy water had dried. The church appeared to be the inside of a tomb, even more porous than the Duomo in Florence. Curtains hung limp in the confessionals. As in Pompei, it seemed these were what remained of a town that had died. There was no air to breathe. Very likely, Johnny thought, the world would choose to end in this place; so dark, so old. Even the light was falling apart.

"One of Papá's ideas is that Mamá's bones be interred in the walls. 'You don't understand these things', Papá told me when I resisted. Can you believe it? Talk to him when we get back, when he is in the mood. But right now, let's go. We're going to be late."

Clearing the jeeps and buses at the intersections, they headed back towards the city. Johnny recognized the houses of some friends; but Martin drove fast, giving him no time to recall names or ask about them. There was one woman who used to visit their mother, bringing grapes and *puto* and, always, terrible news. She wore *saya* and *baro*, like a market vendor, but his mother explained she was as rich if not richer than those who appeared on the society pages of the *Manila Times*. Once, in her black *corchos* and kerchief, she went into Heacock at Dasmarinas and asked to see an emerald brooch. Thinking she was just a poor woman, the salesgirl, one of those *mestizas,* quoted a price without bothering to check, a ridiculously low price which she insisted upon and which the manager then had to honor. Johnny wondered if they had passed her grave in the cemetery.

He felt there was something else he should have done, but he did not know what it was. This made him feel inadequate, an impostor at the clubs where Martin introduced him to strangers as the brother from Boston. The men talked of capital investment declines and an economy short by six percent, of economic stewardship which reduced business confidence because cronies were allowed a free hand, and foreigners permitted to exploit the country in exchange for private deals. Some of the businessmen, Martin explained, had become activists not because of the depressed economy or the growing insurgency that threatened to spread to the city, but the Aquino assassination. Johnny doubted that Martin was one of them.

To Johnny this made no difference. The corruption did not touch him. Though he felt like a little boy being made to perform for his brother's friends, he could take it because he knew it was a one-shot thing. He would not see any of these people again.

Lunch was much too heavy for Johnny. Used to soup and tossed salad or just yogurt, he felt uncomfortable with a meal that was the equivalent of dinner. He began to feel sleepy.

"Keep awake," Martin nudged him between courses.

The beer blurred things for him. He barely saw the people Martin was pointing out to him. Almost four hours since Martin got him out of bed, and he could no longer make any sense out of the conversation. It was two in the morning in Boston. Johnny yawned into his hand. He would give anything to be able to drop into bed.

Martin drove to the restored Intramuros, offered him a tour of the restored house of *hidalgos*. When he showed no interest, Martin just drove around, pointing out new places. "Here is where some people spend their conventions." Martin took him down A. Mabini, past the waiting hostesses.

Bodies hanging out of doorways made no impression on Johnny, who had lost much of his peripheral vision to body-wide fatigue. He could only see the emblem fixed on the hood of Martin's car.

"You probably want to see our new condo site," Martin decided. "Are you in futures, realty, bonds? Any tips I can use?"

Johnny never thought of investments. A paycheck at the end of the month was his idea of security and freedom. Once

31

a month he moonlighted, checking X-ray units for doctors. Occasionally he plunked down a dollar for the Saturday Megabucks, but never bought a daily lottery ticket. That would be increasing his odds of winning. In the back of his mind, he knew it would involve more energy than he had to figure out how to spend a couple of million. And as the jackpot increased the fever grew. It petrified him to imagine himself the winner of 25 million.

"What are you in, Juaniyo?"

"Radiology. Therapy. High intensity Physics."

"Laser?"

"Right. Radiation."

"Is that all?"

"For teaching freshmen physics I share in the college pension fund."

"You're more like Papá than I thought. The type who pays cash. No credit cards, loans, or mortgages. But really, if you get mortgages, the way inflation is eating into the currency, by the time they mature you'll be carrying the amount of your loan in your pocket for one day's expenses. So you get things practically for free. See what I mean, Juaniyo?"

"Johnny," he corrected Martin.

"Okay. Johnny. Just don't be like Papá. Let's round the figures up and say he was doctoring for fifty years. Fifty! Can you believe he retired with only that house? These days, that's the equivalent of retiring with only the shirt on your back. And the old house is shot through with termites. Just waiting to collapse. Like a body eaten up with cancer. Looks good outside but all crumbled inside."

"He seems happy with it."

"That's not the point. Being satisfied is a dead end. I offered to get him a top position when the Heart and the Lung Centers were being set up. He said he could not in good conscience accept such a big salary when so many percent—I forget what figures he quoted—were dying in this country before they're fourteen. Instead of these imposing centers, he said there should be regional establishments where preventive medicine could be practised. Can you believe that? He's upset because the old Quezon Institute is being closed. Tuberculosis has not been eradicated, he says."

"What is the point?"

"We should make more than our parents, own more. Each generation should improve upon the last. Solid investments. Condos are the thing now. After the May elections, if they take place, the condo I'm talking about will double in value. Cash is losing value faster than the tides go out; you'd be gaining if you bought a unit...."

"Investments don't excite me. Was that Cubao we drove through?"

"Wait till you see this place. You're not going to retire in the States, are you? The more people leave, the more will be left for the smart ones who stay. Five hundred meters in Sucat is big enough to sink two million for a modest house. That's pesos. Divide it by seventeen, official rate of exchange—it's twenty-three in the black market...."

"Pure speculation," Johnny recoiled. "I'm not going to clutter the only life I have with mortgage schedules."

"Why not! You've been programmed, Johnny. Emasculated by hopes for Social Security at the end of a working life. Old age is not the time to enjoy life, let me tell you. Look at Papá. Why not experience the high of buying into closed corporations like San Miguel? A ton of cocaine can't give you that, Brother!"

"I'm happy."

"Are you? Well, you can be happier. Look at me. Investments on the West Coast. With you there, I can see myself investing on the East Coast. I have a house in Palm Springs, and a few others. Virginia. Plus others in my name, just as a favor to some friends. You could get into that, too.

33

It pays to own on paper what others cannot own outright without raising questions. If you're interested, I can make the arrangements for you. Then you wouldn't have to teach, or calibrate those X-rays. You could own entire buildings. All you'd have to do is to remember who really owns them. One, I won't tell you his name right now, left for the States with several millions in dollars but he got greedy. They got him. Right in church, too. Someone at communion knelt next to him and shot him with a silencer. Real dramatic."

"Who lives in your houses?"

"Aida has the Palm Beach one. I don't know if you knew we've separated."

"How about the children?"

With Aida. But Martin Junior will be with me when school starts in June. I enrolled him at La Salle."

"Papá knows?"

"Perhaps. But not from me. Maybe he doesn't. I don't get to see him much. I can't ask him to the house. When I call to ask him out, he'd rather not." Martin eases up on the gas pedal in order to confide. "Papá is of Ibarra's generation. It would break his heart to know about Aida and me. He's all virtuous bones. Never strayed from Mamá. She died in his arms, you know. He held her, Salud said, and shouted at the servants to call a doctor. In his panic he forgot—he's the doctor."

Johnny resented the almost casual way Martin was describing their mother's death. Yet where was he when their mother was dying and their father calling frantically for a doctor? Probably caught obscenely inside Rose Quarter. He had had no premonitions, no tug on the heart at the moment of her death, as if he had not grown in her womb.

"Right now, despite what the World Bank may say, this is the place to be, Johnny. As long as you learn to grab your share. If you insist on living abroad, you can hold the

Stateside end of certain investments. You could quit your job right now and simply travel. Don't be alarmed. I won't ask you to carry anything heavy. Papá would enjoy seeing you often. He might even travel with you. *Pa—donker-donker na lang kayo:* don't care! don't care!... It's easy."

Johnny fidgeted. Become a courier? He recalled a news item about gun smuggling from the West Coast that was uncovered by a spot check. Dismantled guns in golf bags. Dollar bills in attaché cases.

"Let's say you make 40,000. Blue Cross/Blue Shield coverage? That and taxes will leave you about 2,500. In the States that will buy you less than it will here. But if you decide to work with us, you'd live like a prince. Summer there. Winter here. Back and forth. Travel to Europe, wherever and whenever you please." Martin drove past a security guard who came forward with a master key.

Johhny had thought of an excuse to return to the hotel. "I'll take a raincheck, Martin. Some other...." He opened the car door to step out before Martin could start the engine again. As he stood up, he saw a tall woman with dark velvety skin starting towards them. Through the thin fabric of her white skirt he saw the sun moving up her inner legs.

Before she reached the car, she stopped, making them come to her while she waited like a cat stretching, unhurried but ready to catch something between her claws.

"The Black Madonna," Martin went to her by way of Johnny, nudging him ahead. "Leticia's sister. Come on. I'll introduce you."

Johnny walked alongside Martin toward the figure that became alternately so small the light could pinch it off and so large that he felt himself being pushed back as he drew closer. He heard music, not far off, but not close to his ear; inside him, riding on the motions of his heart. Nimble, the sound it made pulled him forward.

"Come on," Martin said, hurrying him.

Never in his life had things appeared so clearly and deeply incised. This clarity, however, only painfully separated Johnny from her, making her part of what he could see but not reach: part of that dream where he was running inside his skull.

"My brother, Johnny. I told you about him. The one from Boston. Sylvia Mendez."

She did not say anything, but moved closer to Martin until there was only the thinnest air between them. Johnny wanted her to turn to him, to say something to him and not to his brother, to take his arm and lean on him. He tried to insert his thoughts between them, to pry them apart by wishing, feeling foolish and also helpless, a thirteen year old trying to be the only firefly in the garden.

Because she was tossing her head imperiously in the direction of Martin's mouth, Johnny turned his thoughts to Rose Quarter reclining in bed, as soft as a queen pillow encased in white lace, slipping off another layer of clothing during the TV commercials until by the time the late news came on.... But Sylvia Mendez remained beside Martin, a deliberate echo of every thought he could summon about Rose Quarter, in finer proportion, her dark skin taut as light, giving her loose white dress the excuse of resting against her arms, until all thought of Rose Quarter was stunned out of his head.

Even before Johnny could catch his breath she had said goodbye, nuzzling Martin's cheek so indulgently that Johnny suspected this must be Martin's girlfriend, the one he took to Europe, the one he said he lived with now in the house he had built for Aida and the children. And Martin no longer looked silly in formal *barong* during daytime, not with Sylvia Mendez hanging onto him the way orchids hang on trees in the forest.

Johnny watched her step into her car as if she were being photographed for *Vogue* and heard only every other word

Martin said about another condo in Antipolo: "On the way to *La Nuestra Señora de Buen Viaje,* right smack on a golf course."

Unexpectedly the intensity of his desire for Sylvia Mendez, even before they were introduced, confounded Johnny. He burned slowly with humiliation: was he even in her league, could he have missed her signals that he was not worth her thought? He felt as if a cigarette, lit end inside his mouth, were dropping ashes on his tongue.

Sylvia Mendez was at Leticia's when Martin's chauffeur pulled up at the door to drop them off. Johnny's heart turned loops on seeing her, but he managed to reach for a handshake with an almost steady hand.

Leticia, Martin's live-in, but in another house, took the hand Johnny extended toward Sylvia, rubbed cheeks with him as if they had met before or were family. "You must be Johnny Manalo. Are you back for good?"

Though every bit as stunning as Sylvia—taller and fair, almost white—Leticia did not spark Johnny's interest. Lipstick that only partly covered Leticia's large mouth— from a distance and to someone with poor eyesight she appeared to have a rosebud mouth—coarsened her face for him. He looked around her to Sylvia Mendez who had walked away to stand before a mirror, full length in his thoughts.

As he started toward her, Sylvia moved on, so that Johnny felt wounded, unable to recall anything brave about himself. It was the second time she had ignored him. Outright rejection, no less. From the angle where she stood, it was possible she was looking in his direction, but he could not bring himself to walk the rest of the way.

Who does she love? Johnny Manalo wondered, while a man shook his hand and asked by way of a greeting if he thought Mondale would be nominated by the Democrats. Who does she allow to love her? Another question posed itself in place of a reply, and she stepped into his memory of Rose Quarter reclining on a large white pillow, her short cropped hair tightly curled; he nibbling her ear, her mouth slowly opening, letting out words that bubbled like air, a slow-motion bloom caught by stillness.

Another handshake and more questions he did not bother to understand before replying, "Perhaps." He had not met any of the people who were supposed to be in Boston, either studying or practising their professions. The long-drawn-out questions allowed the guests to clip their vowels like newscasters. Trendy and younger than he, or older but richer, their questions changed the angle of the room.

If he started talking mergers and deficits, reformist pressures from the business sector to curb the presidential decree-making power, would Sylvia Mendez come over?

"Cheers." Someone approached with a glass for him and information that Elizalde was missing and so were twenty-three tribal virgins under his Ministry's charge.

"Cheers." Johnny lifted the glass in a toast, waiting for the code that would break the message apart and disclose its meaning. Unelaborated, this news meant nothing to him.

Someone else observed, "I would not be surprised if the Minister is on his way to a numbered account in Switzerland, heading there in a yacht. Would you? The government has not run out of ingenious ways to siphon off official funds for investments abroad. Did you hear about the buildings in New York City, estates along the Hudson, stud farms in Virginia? If the news ever breaks out, I would not be surprised if we begin hearing talk of impeachment."

Others were eager to pile up more information on Johnny Manalo to see where his loyalties lay. Soon, he was talking in their accent. Rose Quarter used to say, "I can tell when you have been with Filipinos, Johnny. Suddenly all your vowels are broad and long and I can't understand what the hell you're saying.''

If he began talking about the boat he was buying, would Sylvia Mendez come? Or only laugh and call it a washtub? He imagined she would know owners of cruisers with gold bullion in their holds.

"Stay long enough to join a demonstration," someone suggested, going on to describe matrons on marches with servants holding up umbrellas against the sun and old gentlemen in pre-war style jackets and white shoes.

Would Sylvia Mendez laugh at the boat he planned to anchor off Charlestown? Johnny wondered, looking over an ice carving of a *banca* around which floated orchids.

"It occurred to me," a man came over to confide, "that Ninoy escaped the Plaza Miranda bombing—either he was late or never intended to appear—only to get it twelve years later to the day at the airport. Some slow-coming bullet, wouldn't you say? The government's arsenal contains fantastic weaponry. Have you attended the Fact-Finding Board's investigations? Magsaysay Hall, SSS. It's the biggest show in town. You have to be there before it opens in order to get a seat." The man winked. "I mean, before the doors are unlocked for the public, all the seats are filled with government employees, especially from National Intelligence. I think other dictators could learn a lot from ours. Actually, it's the President on trial. The way I see it, the facts have to exonerate him, so the defendants will not be found guilty."

Johnny lost Sylvia Mendez. To keep up with her, he might have to invest in realty as heavily as his brother. The trouble was that he invested in dreams.

"Martha's Vineyard?" Someone's eyebrows lifted when Johnny mentioned the island in response to a question he misheard. "That's the group of Catholic matrons who work with the disabled, not a resort." Unnerved by the association,

Johnny clammed up. He felt like someone waking up repeatedly from different dreams.

"Are you for participation or boycotting the elections? I'm for boycott, but I will register to boycott so no one can vote my name. My youngest son, not quite seventeen, has volunteered to work for free elections with NAMFREL. He said he'll chain himself to a ballot box to keep it from being stuffed with fake ballots or being destroyed. I can't understand him. I give him all the advantages money can buy but he's not interested."

Johnny now discovered Sylvia Mendez standing across the room on her spiked heels and thin but finely-shaped legs. In another instant she had walked through the front door, and a space had opened in the middle of the room. It appeared to Johnny that the guests were making a beeline for the man wheeling himself in—attendants followed at a distance—whose way of propelling himself forward was very much a strut.

"Martin," the man called and Martin came instantly, as if he had been waiting for a command.

Johnny wrestled with his thoughts until his attention latched on to a man wearing a white polo shirt with bright lettering: "You are not alone". Instead of reaching for a handshake, the man turned about to give Johnny a look at his back: a likeness of George Hamilton.

That had to be explained to Johnny, who also puzzled—but not as long—over the next joke. "This is one of the latest: Ninoy walks past Saint Peter at the Gate of Heaven. Seeing Galman, he asks, 'Rolly, why did you shoot me?' Galman looks surprised. 'I didn't do it. I got here ahead of you.' "

"Who's he?" Johnny asked in reply, tipping his head toward the man in the wheelchair.

"That's Walter."

"Walter who?"

"Our host. Leticia's husband. Better or bitter half is everybody's interest and anybody's guess." The man in the white polo was anxious to tell another joke.

Johnny felt drawn to the man in the wheelchair. Not curiosity, but some compelling need demanded he stand close enough to be noticed. Trumpets might have sounded. But it was only a man with a soft pale face that gave the impression of a smile when he was not smiling, a man answering questions in monologue, replying out of turn. The smiles on the guests flashed like the blinking of flashbulbs. Johnny was waiting for his turn when he caught sight of Sylvia Mendez walking by.

"You're not staying for the movie?" Leticia touched Johnny on the arm. "This one was shown at the Manila International Film Festival."

"Porno is meant to be seen on the sly, not along with a hundred other panting hearts," the man with the George Hamilton shirt held Leticia by the waist. "I couldn't stand the Spanish porno films on Texas TV, knowing a million others were watching. Three is the ideal audience. The extra person is for intrigue...."

Sylvia Mendez was not at the front door when Johnny got there, passing by the guests who each asked if he had seen the movie before. Johnny walked down the steps and Martin's driver, recognizing him, came up to ask if he wanted to be taken somewhere.

"Silahis Hotel," Johnny replied, allowing himself to be driven off though he had no such intention in his mind. Beyond the gate which immediately closed after the car, he wondered if Sylvia was back in the garden waiting; if he might order the car turned around without looking like a fool.

Already he was thinking of them as lovers fighting to keep alive their love by filling it with hurt. Without tensions and anxieties the most ardent emotions were supposed to turn wearisome. With Rose Quarter, it was the futility of knowing how she felt about him, what she felt, that intensified his interest, though this had nothing whatever to do with how he saw himself as a person.

He sat impassively in the car, drawing every breath hesitantly, while he imagined scene after scene of pursuit and retreat: in a field of black-eyed susans, in the esplanade along the Hatch Shell, the Fenway—wherever he had been—he altered every episode with Rose Quarter to replace her with Sylvia Mendez. His thoughts partook of the color of green and white *hostas*, the flowering of appletrees, the prick of sand and the fragile sounds of endearment. Her initials might as well have been monogrammed on his chest.

The desk clerk intercepted him on the way to the elevator. "Message, sir." A slip of paper passed between their hands.

Johnny Manalo hurried away to open the note in the privacy of his room but once in the elevator, alone, he was unable to postpone his expectations. What could she want?

"I want to see you. Father." He turned the note over once and again, but the words remained the same.

"He's asleep," the boy met Johnny at the gate of his father's house, holding it almost closed the way his father had done when he had arrived unannounced.

Can it be serious? Johnny wondered, pushing himself against the gate, forcing entry. He could think only of emergencies or crises. Someone dying? Had Rose Quarter called—how would she track him?—telling everything? Or did his father, finding out about Leticia and Martin, want a confirmation?

As soon as Johnny entered the house, he looked out of the window toward the dark street, recalling as he stood there that he had done exactly the same on Friday. A bulb, so low in wattage that it burned like a candle going out, lit the vines that covered the gate. It filled him with longing he could not identify or trace.

Bulbs of the same wattage lit up the sitting room. He did not remember the house ever that dark and sad. The dimness made him think of the turn-of-the-century Italian movie which opened into the interior of a village church where a child was being baptized by candlelight. The muted light, the wrenching color of dried blood made him feel he was being shown the inside of a human body.

He sat down where he had sat the day before, looked up the way he recalled he had on Friday. The same sequence of corners and windows, the particularity of their presence in the room made him think of a wake. Would it be that way when his father died?

The sound of the young boy coughing brought Johnny's thoughts back just as they were turning to Leticia and her party. It seemed to be a movie set where the director could shout, "Cut!" at any minute to bring everyone back to their usual selves. He looked up at the clock above the door to the clinic, checked the time against his watch. Saturday, 11 p.m. No wonder he was starting to hallucinate. He had been up a total of nineteen hours.

He could not decide whether to return to the hotel—he had already dismissed the taxi—or to sleep in his room. He was one hour short of two full days home.

"Can I get you anything?" the boy asked, standing below the Sacred Heart, his face as expressionless as that of an altar-boy concentrating on the Mass.

Johnny shook his head, impressed by the almost kindness in the voice, asking in the manner of Salud who thought food was uppermost in people's minds. "Aren't you sleepy?" Johnny asked the boy who looked bright-eyed as if he needed no sleep.

The boy shook his head, appeared anxious to do something for Johnny. "We cleaned the clinic this afternoon. The doctor and I. We're going to throw out everything that is no longer necessary.''

"Oh?" Johnny made the boy feel important by stopping to listen. "So you have been busy helping my father." He opened the door to the clinic, switched on the light. He stepped on the floor of white tiles, as prim as lace that had been starched to stiffness, and displayed on store windows. He looked about. There were glass cases with stoppered vials, a white sheet over the examining table, the swivel chair, a metal lamp that antique collectors might fight over. Another switch turned on the ceiling fan.

He walked over to the window. The smell of *camia* came up past the iron grilles at the window, and a feeling of sadness swept over Johnny. It felt as if the room, the house, could be lifted up and folded, put away.

Where in that clinic was the child born? Was the message about that?

The thought darkened the room for him. The ceiling dropped as the fan whirred. At a distance from the examining table he tried to imagine the child but could not complete the picture in his mind. A foul taste impossible to swallow filled his mouth.

"Get me a taxi," he turned to the boy who was watching him from the door of the clinic. "Right away."

The boy obeyed instantly, pulling the front door so gently that the only noise heard was the lock sliding into place.

Johnny wished the boy had lingered so he could have changed his mind. It was late, for one thing, and the boy was too young to be out. But perhaps he knew his way, was used to being in the street at any time. He could be older than he appeared to be. Perhaps ten, at least nine, old enough to be careful. Johnny went outside to wait. It should take a few minutes at the most.

A light wind pressed the branches. No lily caught the faint light from the street or the lone bulb at the gate.

Nineteen hours without sleep. Going on twenty. That must be some kind of record.

Somewhere a dog barked, then whined. They used to have dogs and when they whined like that, Salud would make them stop. She said it meant someone dying somewhere. He did not believe her. The dogs used to come rushing when he got home. Halcon, Hero, Horatio were the names until finally his father had only one dog at a time, always Halcon then. One was a runt no higher from the ground than a child's ruler. Another could place his paws on his father's shoulders. Johnny wondered where in the garden the ones he knew were buried. Martin taught them to roll over and beg. His father fed them the best bits on his plate....

Not in the way he appeared or talked, but rather in the way he stood, Martin reminded him of Rick Fielder, for whom Johnny did research at the College. It was not that Rick's reputation could not be supported by his own talent, but Rick used his talent to devise means, ingenious and often extreme, to deny that he was up for retirement. Fielder was good at getting what he wanted—a contract that he could retire at seventy—and better still at getting others to work for him. He threw tantrums and faked heart attacks to get Johnny to cover his classes, to update his research, to attend his conferences and write his papers while Rick stalked the singles bars. Every damn report Rick gave either came from Johnny's idea or Rick's idea developed by Johnny. Three years running, Rick had received the best teacher award with a thousand-dollar salary increment on the basis of Johnny's efforts.

It had begun to gall. Especially when Johnny discovered that Rick was not putting in a good word for him at the faculty boards. But Rick had guessed about the fake marriage and confronted Johnny with it outright. Johnny had not yet learned to lie. So Rick Fielder had it made.

The only thing Johnny would not allow Rick Fielder was to lay his fat fingers on him. Other students, male and female, did allow it, for no more than a B-minus. Bugger, bugger, Johnny Manalo pronounced the words, working up an anger to get rid of feelings he could not name.

No clear and certain words could declare what he felt, which he tried to walk off at night: from Davis Square to Harvard through Porter Square, to Inman through Central and round about to Brattle; just walking about casually, catching glimpses of families at dinner or sitting in front of television; of hamburgers being flipped at cafés, people browsing through books: faces he rarely caught exchanging expressions. He walked until he felt light and free inside, the blood running, but no longer furiously through clenched veins.

He never wanted anything he saw. But he wanted something, wanted it without hurry, almost certain it would come as long as he outlasted its coming. It was not indifference, for it was a struggle with all the body's hungers intact.

An hour passed. No longer sleepy, he opened the gate to look up and down the street. Both ways it was darkness. Headlights from the main road, ten houses down on either side of the road, drew him out. He pulled the gate shut and began walking. If he met the boy, he would tell him to forget it, to go home. He would get his own taxi.

There were lights behind closed windows of the houses he passed. Trees and vines covered them from prying eyes. He looked back towards his father's house. Above it he thought he saw a star, but it might have been a plane. When he was a boy, at night after all the patients had gone, unable to eat, his father would walk around the block, a fast walk that kept Johnny running to keep up. He recalled once stepping high over what he thought was wire strung on the ground. It turned out to be just the overhead wire's shadow.

There was a moon. That and his father's whistling covered up his embarrassment. He wanted to remember more but there was nothing else.

Cutting short its route, a jeepney came rushing down the road out of the main street, throwing Johnny's shadow far ahead, then upright against the fences before dropping him back into darkness. It was as if he had been spotlighted and for some reason that reminded him of trying to catch Sylvia Mendez at her sister's house where she had simply walked out into the garden. His effort to find her had been half-hearted.

Hands in his pockets, he tried to whistle. He could not decide on an appropriate tune, remembered that he rarely whistled. A friend from grade school, the Apostol Elementary, could whistle Christmas carols. His father worked in Hawaii, visited once a year and during illnesses. They borrowed each other's comics, sometimes shared snacks. So much for young attachments. He could not recall more than that, yet he felt close to that friend, had wanted him to be his brother.

Salud kept an eye on their young friendships, while she walked them to school and back. No one was good enough for him and Martin. Nothing was good enough for them either. While other children ran to the stores during recess and after classes, Salud brought them soup. It was embarrassing to have her feed them under the *mabolo* tree while their schoolmates fed themselves ricecakes, slices of fruit that had been soaked in salted water or ice drops: all of which Salud classified as dirty. "Your father would get angry if he found out I let you."

They were not allowed to buy food peddled down the street. From their gate he remembered waiting for the vendors who stopped regularly at the other houses, uncovering with the same hands that accepted money and gave out change the flat baskets of *puto* or fried bananas, *palitao* or *okoy*. Their smells were familiar to him.

Johnny didn't suppose children's brains ever curdled from eating peddled food and dirty ice cream.

He did not recall ever fighting with that friend. If they had fought, he would have had more to remember. Psychologists said conflicts were natural and necessary in every friendship. Agitation sustained interest. Discord made love awesome. He and Sylvia Mendez were off to a blazing start.

Rose Quarter and he made no difference to each other. Though avoidance created a sustaining tension, he and Rose Quarter, from the very first time, pushed ahead to conclusion. His. She had let him come.

However, Johnny suspected that all over the world relationships ended in disappointment, and not for any particular reason. The chaplain at the College, who was also curate at Our Lady of Pity, said that this was from trying to replace God with people, with goods and other passing interests. "We will never be content with one another while we push Him out of our relationships. Because He is part of every friendship, every love affair. He is the part that is constant and faithful."

Why those words would follow him to his father's place when they had slid off him during the sermon, follow him intact, when he had never thought of them before—he could not explain. He was a fringe Catholic who went to church on high holy days, genuflected before entering, knew the standard prayers but no longer said them. He had received First Communion with his father and his mother—in a wheelchair—watching. But he never thought those moments had anything at all to do with God, really. They were rites of passage, rituals to entice his father out of his clinic, the sanitized equivalent of being circumcized in the woods.

The end of the street, both corners, were empty. Where

had the boy gone? A taxi with occupants passed by. Jeepneys and a bus coasted along, picking up passengers.

Johnny decided to walk toward the Monument where it would be easier to hail a taxi. The boy must have wandered off. That late—it was almost Sunday—there was no excuse for him not to have returned to the house if he could not get a taxi.

An old woman sat in the shadows of a closed store. Before her was a tray of cigarettes, a few coughdrops—yellow and green wrappers. Beside her a little child was asleep on the pavement. In Boston it was unthinkable to see people without shelter. Those on Welfare complained about government housing that would be luxurious to many in Manila. There were occasional bag ladies, of course, and old men who carried everything they owned on them, with their clothes in layers, sleeping on park benches or in subways. It was still worse in New York.

He passed other vendors on the sidewalk. Short stubs of candles lit up their wares: *balut*, *mais*, mangoes already pared inside plastic bags, sliced and salted. A watch repair shop occupied the space of a stool. It was no more than an upright cubicle with a glass front. Fastfood restaurants, barbershops, variety stores, optometrists, pharmacies filled with people waving prescriptions to get the attention of clerks, moviehouses with air conditioning spilling out onto the sidewalk where people dallied to look up at the escalator and the posters of coming attractions, pizza and hamburger places with soft-drink cases pre-empting the public walking space, *lechon* and *chicharon* counters, department stores displaying pale mannequins dressed in floral prints with limbs arranged in arrested flight; cubicles too dark for youths to read the rental comicbooks engrossing them, frayed pages clipped to the walls on wires. The side-by-side assortment distracted and bewildered Johnny Manalo.

He walked slowly past more of the same, tempted by

peanuts heaped in baskets, ice drops and ice cream sold from carts, corn still being roasted out in the open—wherever there was space to set up portable or makeshift grills—not because he was hungry but because it seemed the one way to be part of the scene.

Not in years had he seen so many people per square foot. The press of crowds in buses, sidewalks and stores overflowed every bit of space. Where did they sleep and when?

He stopped in front of a pile of what looked like marshmallows browned on sticks. "What are those?" he asked, tempted. "Day-old chicks roasted fresh." He hurried away, looking to neither side.

On the other extensions from the rotary formed by Bonifacio's Monument—like tubes terminating in a chamber—there was the same congestion of space and senses, the contemporary limits of man's aspirations.

The juxtaposition of ragged clothes and fashion jeans, of bodies bent under loads carried all day and those springing erect and high like wheat panicles, of need that survived on selling gum by the stick and of means that allowed the purchase of the same cosmetics sold on Boston's wealthy Newbury Street—it seemed to Johnny a kind of violation.

He could not tell what the situation demanded of him. The disparities mocked him. Partaking of the proportions of nightmares, the waters standing in the heaved-up concrete, the peels and wrappers that coalesced under the stream of pedestrians, the darkness that began at the tip of lights gave Johnny the feeling of being in an inferno, a prelude to dissolution. He thought of Goya's monstrous mouths stuffed with human bodies, the faces decaying in full view, corpses standing up to firing squads: everywhere the coarse imprint of death's celebrations.

Back in his hotel room with early Sunday entering into daylight, Johnny Manalo waited for something to squelch the alarm that had been triggered in him. Against the wall of fighting cocks—another death disassembling its apparitions—he recalled blackbird droppings along with red berries of the dogwood below his attic window, recalled the white dogwood flowers imprinted with the crucifixion.

It had been thirty-three hours straight before he fell asleep. The telephone rang. "Try calling at a decent hour," he snapped into the receiver, dropped it but missed the cradle, so that he heard incoherent music and laughter, and his name being called: Johnny.

Something in the way he heard his name made him think of a cat stretching in the sun, of someone under the sheet, sliding against him. He reached for the phone but it dropped to the floor and was silent.

With no way of calling back, Johnny leaped out of bed as if to rush after the voice, follow it through the streets to claim it.

The two fighting cocks, claws sunk in the walls and staked in place by the raised arms of *aficionados*, sobered him. Instead of hurling things about, he sat down at the side of the bed. Watching the combat fixed on the wall began to calm him. His feelings settled.

If it was Sylvia Mendez who had called, why? The very idea that it was she stirred up pleasant memories he had not had with her.

A second time Johnny fell asleep, breathing free of himself until his dream of climbing and lifting himself over walls was intercepted by Rick Fielder/Rose Quarter who were racing each other to him, intent on pulling Sylvia Mendez away.

And a second time he woke up. It was the desk clerk

ringing to say a Mr. Manalo was on the way to his room. It's about time Martin came to see where I went, Johnny thought, opening the door, then stripping down to his shorts on the way to shower.

He would make his brother wait.

Full force he turned on the water to drown out his own misgivings in the lukewarm slush. It was he who had simply taken off without leave either from Leticia or Martin. And was not his host, Walter, to be considered also?

"I'll just be a minute. Take a seat," Johnny called through the door when he heard someone enter. "Take a seat."

It was his father, not Martin. Not expecting this, Johnny felt exactly as he did when he had come to his father's house empty-handed.

"I'm sorry," Johnny said, with no specific transgression in mind. He cleared the armchair of his clothes, pulled and pushed it toward the window. When he drew the drapes aside he was suprised. Daylight struck him from the sea. It was afternoon. "What day is it, Papá?"

"Sunday, *Hijo*. I didn't think you were asleep or I would not have come up."

"Still Sunday? It's all right, Papá. I'm glad you got me up. I did get your message last night and I came, but you were asleep."

"I thought it was you. Martin is not in the habit of visiting and I saw this on the coffee table."

It was the message the desk clerk had given him.

"I'm here because of the boy, Rio. He was not there when I got up this morning. He usually has water heating and the *pan de sal* on the table. It's not like him to leave without asking permission, so I thought you might have brought him along."

Johnny recalled he had asked the boy to get him a taxi but it was not something he wanted to admit. Yet he had nothing to say in its place. "Can I have breakfast brought

52

up, Papá? Beer? Coffee? Let me change and we can go down to the restaurant."

"I've had breakfast and lunch, *hijo*. I won't stay. You're busy."

"Things can wait, Papá." It became urgent that his father stay. "Have a seat. I can be ready in a minute."

"I have to look for the boy. He did not even lock up. That's strange, knowing him. Thieves could have broken in while I slept. I have to check with his mother. I didn't want to, unless I have to."

"She would know where he is. He probably went home."

"She asked me to take him in so he can get three meals a day and go to school at Apostol. She's afraid of their place. There are drug pushers, recruiters of every kind. New People's Army, she says. Military dragnets constantly harass the squatters...."

"Do you think he ran away? Or perhaps, something...." Johnny thought of possibilities they could discuss to keep his father there. He felt powerless to make him stay; a child again, a child who had climbed up a tree and could not come down on his own.

His father did not reply, but started for the door. "After your convention, *hijo*, we'll get together. I have not had a good *kare*, as good as Salud made, in a long time. Before you leave, I'll find someone who can cook curry the same way we used to have it. Don't see me out. Go back to sleep."

There was no way he could have kept his father there, short of standing in his way. It was as if his father and he had met in a dream.

Sylvia Mendez simply stood in his way in the lobby, up from a sidechair. "Hello," she said. "I was the one who called. Are you awake now?"

Johnny Manalo fumbled for something awesome to say.

But, discarding all ideas as they came to him, he was reduced to smiling.

"So you're not going to say something to me. Don't use that convention excuse with me, Johnny Manalo. First, it's Sunday. And since that bomb blew up the International Travel Agents Convention, with Marcos at the podium, the Convention Center has not been booked except for weddings. So, you might as well take me to lunch."

"Where?"

"Here. The *tanguingue* steak is good at Capriccio." And she led him to the restaurant while he followed, his attention on the white plunge of her dress that ended in the small of her back.

The headwaiter sat them beside some palms, on plush chairs. Obscured somewhat, Johnny still felt he had been seated in the open, and waited to see what else would happen.

She ordered some drink with a long winding name, and *tanguingue* steak for him. "With lime juice," she told the waiter. "Freshly squeezed!"

The drink was rough in his throat like the burning dance of a laser. It surprised another smile out of him. She is no Rose Quarter, he thought, now wary about Sylvia Mendez, for she appeared capable of suddenly changing—the way protons broke orbit around their nuclei.

An arm's length from Sylvia, Johnny took refuge from the possibilities by thinking deliberately of Rose Quarter who, wearing flat shoes, stood head to head with him, a large soft petal with blue eyes when she smiled and gray, like steel, when she sulked. When she beamed, Rose could outshine Christine Brinkley in a bikini, but a virtuoso like Martin would never stop to give her his little finger.

One hand resting on her shoulder against the neck, Sylvia Mendez watched Johnny as if processing his every thought through her mind. "I have not decided about you," she was saying.

He could not put words together in any order. He could only look back, not directly but on her lips as she spoke.

"I don't know if I like you. I know I don't like your brother. Are you married?"

Her question made him feel as if beams delivering 100 trillion watts each had simultaneously hit him; he was vaporizing under the pressure. No part of his mind could escape her sitting there, waiting for his answer.

The fish steak was brought out flaming on a wooden platter and placed before him.

"Tell me if it's good," she said, leaning forward. "And you can call me *Preciosa*. Everyone does, family or friend. We're kind of family aren't we? At least with Leticia and Martin hot for each other at the moment."

Her dark skin silky soft, the curls loose all over her head, gave the impression that she was disrobed. He could not bear to look at her, or look away.

"Is it good?"

He cut at the tip of the *tanguingue* carefully, speared a portion with the fork and was bringing it to his mouth when she opened hers, unfurling her tongue between her lips so that he had to place the morsel upon it. She pulled the fish off with her teeth, leaving the fork smeared with lipstick.

"Not as good as they say," Syliva Mendez said, getting up. "Come on. There's another place."

And Johnny Manalo followed her once more, showing the waiter the room number on his key as they hurried away. Stepping out into the sun after her, Johnny felt caught in the pulsing of light, a thousand times brighter than sunlight, felt he was about to be fused, shut out of his old life. He was happy and grateful.

While she drove she stopped speaking, racing ahead silently

as if presenting the city to him through a succession of mirrors. She even yawned at intersections, waiting for the light to change on Taft. Concrete forms crossed the avenue. He remembered one rainy day when he was still at the University of the Philippines, somewhere on that avenue near the Philippine General Hospital he had almost stepped into an uncovered manhole during the flood. And again, another flood through which his car would not drive; he recalled coming home down Rizal Avenue, walking under the electric poles to guide himself. Only when he reached home did he realize how lucky he was not to have touched live wires brought down by the wind.

How that series of lucky situations brought him side by side with Sylvia Mendez in her red Mercedes puzzled him. There must be a pattern to life after all, a purpose. But what, in his case?

"Did I say that?" she was asking and he had no idea what she meant. Dodging jeepneys, buses and cars, she sped in and out of the standing concrete posts as if trying to surprise the future.

"Why don't you like my brother?" Johnny Manalo asked, obliged to ask a question so it would not seem that she was talking to herself. It was the one thing she had said that he remembered.

Sylvia Mendez looked off to her left. Fiercely red nail polish bloomed on her nails. She did not reply to his question.

Johnny did not insist. After all, he had not heard what she must have referred to in the beginning. And he really did not have a right to inquire into her feelings. But he wondered if she kept track of what she said.

"See that?" She looked up at the concrete beams overhead. "Madame is providing the city with a light rail system. Zoom to your destination while ordinary traffic plods below. You can't imagine how much in kickbacks the project represents. And your brother, thinking small as usual, tried to get snack concessions at the exits and entrances. He should have known food would be banned on the system. We Filipinos eat too much and throw wrappers and peeling indiscriminately. Can you imagine driving underneath and getting corn husks or banana peels thrown at your windshield?''

If that was the reason she did not like Martin, it sounded superficial, so there had to be a real reason she was taking time to throw at him.

She cast a look at him, then pulled a sigh from deep in her lungs and waited for air to return to her body. ''He can never be another Walter. Walter is conglomerates and mines and insurance and shipping and banks, logging and fishing, processing plants, export zones, tobacco.... Everything big. Coconut....You know what? He's one of the select few who determine the dollar exchange rate. Even if the Malacañang pair skim 10% off the top, Walter has millions left. Can you keep a secret? He's into investments. All the overseas ones. Martin is just an errand boy. Of course many government people also run errands for the Chief. But Walter is the full partner. He has everything.''

So it was a comparison game. Having expected a worse reason not to like his brother, he was relieved. In case Sylvia Mendez recalled she had not identified her hero, he asked, ''Who's Walter?''

''Leticia's husband, of course.''

''Oh,'' he said.

''Do odd couples bother you, Johnny? Everyone knows about her and Martin. God knows. He has not intervened. Guess, is she older than I am?''

He could not tell, but he guessed in her favor. ''Older.''

''It's hot, isn't it. If the aircon doesn't blast icy, it's Sahara hot. The car is from Walter. I should tell him it's not behaving, so he can get me another. I can afford it, on my own,

Johnny. Don't jump to the wrong conclusions. It's just that Walter likes to give gifts. If you refuse, he gets offended."

And Martin, Johnny asked himself. What did his brother give?

"Didn't you see Walter at the party?"

He lied, "No."

"He was the one in the wheelchair. He must have wheeled himself out again. He can't stand people pressing close to him. There were Unified Field people...."

"What's that?"

"Maharishi stuff. They came to ask him for support. The First Couple have been persuaded to be First Mother and First Father of Enlightenment. Patron. Patroness. Those *gurus* are playing it extra safe and sought Walter for a First Uncle." She laughed. "I can see you don't have a *guru*, Johnny. You look pretty confused."

"Do I?"

"Would you say that Leticia is kindhearted?"

He had not anticipated that question. It required more judgment than could come from a quick meeting, and he could not tell what had compelled her to ask.

"No opinion, Johnny? I'll tell you. Leticia is a hot pickle. Her Maria Clara manners turn men on, but...she's my sister after all. You'll misunderstand what I say."

"No, I won't." He was more than curious. Surely, from the proper perspective, everything she said must add up.

"Are you sure you don't know? Has Martin said nothing?" "No."

"Well. Walter was forty when he started coming to the house, dead set on marrying one of Papá's daughters. That must have been twenty, twenty-five years ago. Leticia said yes. Papá had to be persuaded. It took a year. Leticia wanted to be married in high style. Then she became restless. The houses were not enough. The trips and the jewels. Having more than any of us became boring. She started having

58

parties. Politicians, ambassadors, businessmen, ministers. She likes everyone. She likes you, too. And Walter, of course, has his own wandering eye, his own playmates. But he's a man.''

Wouldn't he know it—she believed in the double standard.

"Walter saw you at the party. He asked who you were. I said you're a scientist from Cambridge. He's impressed. The only academics he has met so far are too concerned with human rights. But Walter likes you, he said.''

Johnny did not know how to act flattered, didn't know if Sylvia Mendez was lying. Speaking might be her way of keeping him at a distance. Any word would do. The more meaningless the connections, the better to keep them apart. Or she might be trying to connect.

"Walter has this building. Seven floors in Binondo. I've never seen it. His mother is on the top floor. The street level is rented out—you know, shops. In between are apartments for his mistresses. Three is his lucky number, so his favorite is on the third floor. Besides that, he's always on the prowl. In his wheelchair, no less. The candidates for Miss Philippines go for him. And so on, and so on, *ad nauseam*. They deserve one another, don't you think?''

He could not think. There were ten things she had thrown at him. Even if he could sort them out to which should he respond? He was beginning to feel once again that he was in a target chamber for laser beams.

"Martin is her latest. But I don't expect him to last. She's already talking about Mexico City. She goes there to get her emotional divorces. Should I perhaps say spiritual?''

"I don't know," he answered. It depended on whether she meant affections, or something more sacred. Maybe neither.

"Money never interested me—having it or making it. One could rob a bank or get a rich lover, but not for the money.

59

It's just an excuse. Until Letts finds another man, she and Walter, you'd think seeing them that they're young sweethearts.... He's at least two hundred and fifty pounds and ailing all over. He goes to faith healers. Before he became crippled, he went to European clinics. Now a doctor from Switzerland comes to give him shots. When Walter's pumped full of drugs he acts crazy. Afterwards, he doesn't remember anything. He could have you killed and the next day ask for you. He has no memory of what he has done. Martin is one of his *tutas*. I don't think you can be a puppy, Johnny. Can you lick hands?''

He weighed his answer. But before he could speak, as if she already knew what he would say or did not care, Sylvia pointed out the Monument. ''Now, you can say you've seen Tolentino's sculpture. The angel on top, doesn't it....I'd better not. I have a feeling you're a prude, Johnny. Are you? You have not relaxed a bit since you got in my car. Do you think I've kidnapped you or something?'' She stopped right in the middle of the Avenida Rizal Extension to accuse him. Behind them cars and buses and jeepneys were blasting their horns.

It felt to Johnny as if it were thundering and storming, that they were time encapsulated: two planets circling a center that no longer existed.

No fewer than twenty, all young and intense, were waiting on the front porch of Sylvia Mendez' house in Santa Mesa. Intricate grillwork at the windows and doors, a long outside stair more proper to the interior of a castle severely dated it, yet also made it appear to be built on air. The last thing Johnny expected was for her to live in a house crowned by spreading acacias, hedged-in by old-fashioned hibiscus and clumps of gardenia, all of which were so out of keeping with the contemporary spareness of her body, her abrupt silences and declarations.

Johnny followed her up the stairs, on pink polished tiles. Those waiting came down as they went up.

"Have you decided?" Their several voices posed one question. "Sylvia. Say you have. Say yes."

Sylvia glided up like a dark lily to their center, was lost from his view with the huggings and gestures proper to long-lost friends.

Someone, younger than he and almost as tall, broke away to walk down to where Johnny had stopped on the stairs. "The problem is that the Marcos machine wants her, too. We know what we're up against."

"Really?" Johnny asked, barely interested.

"Her brother-in-law is one of the cronies. He gets his loans from the government practically free. SSS and GSIS funds that should go to the employees for housing go to the select few who pay, if at all, special low rates. With galloping inflation, that means free loans."

Johnny had no reply. He stuffed both hands in his side pockets and dropped his eyes to the tiles where the faded spots were light flower shapes. Exhausting the designs, he looked up and saw the thin roofs of squatter huts through the heavy branches of trees.

"Pete Alvarez," the young man offered him a handshake. "Johnny Manalo." He pulled a hand out slowly, returning it immediately to his pocket.

"I haven't seen you around."

"I just arrived."

"From where?"

Johnny did not answer but turned to face the front door of the house, which Sylvia had ordered open without inviting people in. He saw a piano covered with lace and portraits. No chromo stuff. Green ceramic plant stands held ferns at the corners and beside doors, above which were carved panels that ventilated the rooms. A framed mirror into which leaves were incised. A hatrack of deer antlers above an umbrella stand. He wanted to enter, to touch the objects he had seen from the porch.

Light German beer and San Miguel were brought in bottles along with trays of finger food. The noise level grew. Groups formed and broke away, following no pattern or reason Johnny could detect. The feast was set up in the porch that ran halfway around the house so he could look into the front rooms. Some of the young girls brought their plates to sit on the steps, facing the street. Their legs crossed under their wide skirts.

"Every time we come, she feeds us," Pete Alvarez said, refusing a plate but accepting beer. "Food is not what we come for, but commitment."

A maid passed a plate of multicolored rice cakes. Another followed with spring rolls and *sotanghon*. The transparent noodles tempted Johnny. Sylvia had not taken him to that other restaurant, which she said served better *tanguingue*.

"Sylvia said she'll decide tomorrow. That's what she said yesterday. Yet she knows we need time to mobilize."

"Suppose she refuses," Johnny was already delighted with the possibility. Should he be the only one she rejected?

"Then we'll boycott the May elections for Batasan members. But if she accepts—I'm almost sure she will— then we're prepared to knock on every door to ask people to register on the weekends of the 18th and 25th. At the election, we're prepared to guard the ballot boxes all night to keep them from being stolen."

"It beats having nothing to do, I guess," Johnny said, waiting for the maid to bring a glass into which he could pour the beer, rapidly getting lukewarm in his hand.

"It's not just a matter of keeping busy," Pete answered, obviously offended. "We have all received threats. They alternate with bribes. Some of us have weakened and now work for the government. Others have gone to the hills. But we want to find a moderate alternative to dictatorship and communism.''

He did not mean it the way it sounded, but Johnny was not prepared to apologize. ''Politics is not my game. I try not to meddle.'' He wanted to hear no more about it.

''If you don't resist all the way, you begin to be pulled in. No easy choices about politics. We have to make a stand. Not the stand of those in the States who talk revolution while they draw hefty salaries, safe on their ivory pedestals. Any one of us here could disappear tomorrow. But we also know that someone will take our place.'' Pete's voice softened as he spoke, lost its anger. He sounded almost friendly again. ''Nothing personal, Johnny. But no one can stand aside. Or pay lip service. Here is where the battle is being fought. Now.''

''Does Sylvia Mendez stand a chance?'' Johnny felt he had to be formal and use her full name.

''She's old family, from this neighbourhood. And she's not frightened. Even against the Marcos candidate, she could win big. But she has to put everything into it. Campaign. Not play the socialite who, after a day with the laborers and the poor, retires to her swimming pool. That would only highlight the discrepancies we mean to dissolve. Really. She has to divest herself of her privleges. Become one with the people. I think she can make the sacrifice. It's about time.''

''I'm tired,'' Sylvia Mendez walked over to Pete and Johnny, stretching as if she had just gotten out of bed. ''I can hardly keep awake.''

''We're about to leave anyway,'' Pete Alvarez said. He had been telling Johnny how squatters and the urban poor were chased from place to place by the government, which was embarrassed by their poverty. He set his unfinished bottle of beer on the steps for the maids to pick up.

Sylvia Mendez called into the house, ''Turn on the lights at the gate. They're leaving.''

"Will you let us know right away?" Pete asked.

"Say 'Yes', Sylvia. Run. Show the government what we can do for the country." The others set their plates on the table before turning to go. Young girls rubbed cheeks with Sylvia one more time, startling Johnny at the ease with which they all accepted being asked to leave. What were they prepared to do for Sylvia Mendez?

She walked them out to the gate. "You must come again," she told them, as if they had come on a social call. "Thank you all for coming." Then she stood at the gate, waving until every last one had left, walked away or boarded the jeepneys or the buses.

Through the long way back, past *campanillas* and around the large *macopa* tree too old to be shaped by the wind or turned by the sun any longer, Sylvia Mendez returned to the house, to where Johnny stood halfway down the stairs.

He had stopped sweating. Suddenly it was cool. Air was flowing through the branches covering the rain-soaked sky. He could smell something sweet coming up from the bushes.

She came up to where he stood, her hands behind her back like a little girl reluctantly obeying a summons to come in for the night. She must be all of thirty, Johnny calculated, looking for signs that she was younger. Most probably she was pushing forty if, as she said, she had gone to Marymount and Catholic University, then lived in Mexico City for five years. He could not tell what had made her say all this to him, take the time to tell him about herself, with the young people waiting in the porch.

He could not tell if she wanted him out of the house, too. He hoped not. For as she drifted toward him she could just as well have sprouted wings, so innocent and childlike did she appear that he was soaring through her, wild and free.

For the longest time she stood silent in the porch alongside Johnny, both hands on the railing and looking up at the sky as if the moon hung there in all tenderness.

That was what went through his mind while he watched her, so slight, so small even, for she had slipped off her shoes. It occurred to him that Martin's desertion of his family and his coupling with Leticia, his own sudden decision to come home for a visit, were all part of what had been planned ahead to fulfill some overarching intention against which it was useless to struggle.

Before any person was born, Lacan said, there were already brought together the words that would make him either faithful or a renegade. There were already laws that would follow him to the very place where he had not yet been. And this was even before those who were to love him into life were born.

He wanted to believe in God right then. Out of gratitude he wanted to pray. While standing there beside her on the porch, he felt an intimacy he had not felt with Rose Quarter. Full of longing but determined not to force anything because fulfillment came regardless, he felt unable to act upon his desire to crush her to himself.

Full of words singing, words waiting to be said for the first time, it surprised him to see her suddenly turn and walk into the house, without a word.

Johnny waited for her to come out again, to return to him. It was her driver who came, announcing Sylvia's order to take him back to his hotel: "Sir, Miss Mendez said you can use me tonight if you wish."

Spoken without feeling, the words restrained Johnny's reaction. Immediately, he turned to go; as if that had been his intention all along, as if he wanted nothing else. But still pulsing, his body throbbed with an energy that hurt.

Inadmissible feelings surfaced when Johnny Manalo reached his hotel. Sylvia Mendez had changed right before his eyes and he was left with his burst and wounded self.

With the tap turned up as hot as he could stand it, he stood under the shower, quarreling with his own behavior. Suppose? But he had never supposed with Rose Quarter.

He tried to bring back his confidence by thinking of Rose, but she had receded so far in his memory that no amount of concentration could bring her back. At least, Johnny thought, this thing with Sylvia Mendez happened early and ended just as soon. Now he could go about the business of his visit, with no distractions.

That decision reached, he planned the next steps: check out early Monday morning, move in with his father, back to Boston at the end of the month. That left him twenty-six days. It was long enough to make up to his father for his long absence. And as for Martin, they might or might not run into each other again—same difference.

He would cease to be another of Sylvia Mendez' camp followers. For all he cared, she could scream or whistle, run or not, for Pete Alvarez.

As if he were on some river bottom, the fighting cocks across the room looked muddy on the wall. He turned to the bed. As the first time he entered that room, he noticed the shadows of bodies upon the red pattern of the bedcover. He tried to imagine Sylvia Mendez there. Shit. Even the color of the pillows was vulgar, spoiling everything. How could he feel, no more than five hours before, that he had wanted Sylvia Mendez all his life, that he had found his nerve endings?

It could not be anyone now. Not even Rose Quarter.

He sank into one of the chairs by the window, wondering who might be in the lobby that early. A morning traffic of bright fuchsia shirts with blues and yellows; tourists in tennis shoes and shorts and bulging sandals. Martin said he hated to be seated next to them at the lunches where finely-shaped bodies peeled off on a ramp, turning to surprise the cameras. Johnny remembered maneuvering introductions to such perfumed women, spending one semester's tuition just to be able to get within a whiff of their ears. No such strategies were required in Boston. How about dinner at the Peacock? was enough. It went on from there. The next time, meeting by accident, you could go out to dinner again, or avoid each other's eyes. No promises.

Before he moved in with his father, he had better resolve Rose Quarter, too. Send her a postcard—a *nipa* hut or a sunset motif: So long...thanks for everything. Or: thanks for nothing. A dear-Rose letter. No return address. Morgan Memorial or St. Vincent de Paul could haul away his stuff, and Mary could advertise for a new tenant. He would miss her garden and the red cardinal that rested in the lilacs when it could have chosen the oak. But he could start again in San Francisco. "So long" was a clear enough message.

They might meet by chance and not recognize each other. He knew no more about Rose Quarter than was required to identify her at a morgue. Nothing about why she lived off taking care of Mary instead of finding a job elsewhere. He more than suspected that Mary supported her medication, that Rose was on some prescription to control her thoughts or her emotions. There was always, he felt, the threat of something about to break loose from her, tears or anger, and not necessarily called for by the situation.

His throat was dry. He was always thirsty in bed with Rose Quarter. Thirsty while they stared off at different walls. Once though, he said something and she had smiled open-mouthed, beaming. It was as if something, not what he said, had clicked inside her mind, a thought passing successfully through the field of electricity in her brain, the passing giving her pleasure that delighted her and lifted her out of herself to him.

And yes, he cared. Not meticulous care but concern nevertheless. For example, since he arrived in Manila, he had wondered several times if she continued to swim at the Y.

Because of her thyroid condition, unless she swam regularly she would put on weight. She was already too heavy for her bones.

And he tried to take her to museums and fine restaurants, gifted her with certificates to Filene's, The Coop, Lord and Taylor, so she would dress better and reorder a life that seemed full of stillborn hopes. He brought her to Mystic Seaport, to see the millionaire's cottages in Newport—for which palaces in Europe had been ransacked at the turn of the century—the four floors of memorabilia and art at the Isabela Stewart Gardner and the chapter house in the Worcester Art Museum. She said the tapestries were fading like fingerprints and asked what had happened to the Italian church from which the chapels were removed. He tried to bring her out to feel the real sun in the sky—instead of a tanning lamp—and real sea, instead of those prints of oceans which she had on her walls.

He got her to work on a picture by coloring numbered sections shaped like jigsaw puzzles. She chose one of waves breaking against a cliff, but still had not finished it.

He asked Mary questions that would fill in what he knew of Rose Quarter. Something in her childhood perhaps. What? If Mary and her husband had adopted her, would she have become immobilized like someone blind, trapped in pre-sexual innocence?

Mary thought there was no way to change her. "Life made her that way, Johnny. It's no one's fault. There's just too much grief in her. Could have been born with it. That's why my husband did not adopt her. He wanted to do something for her. I explained the way I am explaining to you, in order to save him the frustration. She can't be helped. We loved her but what can we do, how can we love her, if she does not respond?"

He tried to startle Rose Quarter out of herself, to tempt her to become thin and want what she did not have. When she undressed for him there was no seduction. Just a plain, ordinary, necessary act like washing her face in the morning. She would lie still, moving only to rub against the sheets. He had given up trying to find her center in the dark without touching her.

For she did not like to be touched, or even to be kissed deep, be stroked or warmed by his breath. Words of endearment might be flung, to better result, against a door. She always fell asleep, or made a good imitation of falling asleep before he was through; lying simply free of him while he was still on top of her, still climbing.

An hour a week, every Tuesday, brought seventy-five dollars out of Mary's pocket for Rose Quarter's doctor. This fact came out when Mary said she needed the rent paid in full on the dot, or Rose would miss her visit. Rose Quarter's medication had to be adjusted. Too much or the wrong combination, and she might not wake up. Once, bedded down with arthritis, Mary had called him up to knock at her door: "She has not come down to breakfast, Johnny. It's not like Rose to be late making my tea. See what she's up to, now."

Mary said Rose Quarter liked him. Also that she would be childlike always. "But she's good with plants. Weeds bloom as large as annuals for her. If I can only get her to plant astilbes and cleomes...."

For some time he believed that if Rose Quarter had someone she loved, who could make her want to, she would become a butterfly instead of a moth. In the back of his mind, the reason he was giving her time, being gentle about the divorce, was that, if brought up too abruptly, it might push her over the edge. She might take all her pills in one swallow.

If he had known from the beginning. If he had pieced together all the things he knew. Or if he had not been touched by her gentleness, her lack of any defensive mechanism. Part of Johnny still wanted to lead her out into the sunlight. Part, however, suspected she was different in unseen ways as well, that all the feelings she showed were as much as he would get out of her, ever.

Despite her imperfections, in the absence of lust or rage, and with the sense of failure she gave him, it was her simple goodness—locked in the changeless prism of her mind and heart, obscured by her moods and inarticulateness—that might just stun him out of lies.

Yet, if he understood this much about Rose Quarter, could he be that well himself?

"By any chance do you live on Prentiss Street?" A short thin man with brown corduroy trousers that ended some way above blue argyle socks, a dazzling white *barong* with pockets, came up to Johnny Manalo while he was checking out Monday morning. Thick glasses magnified his eyes which seemed loose in their sockets.

"Prentiss Street?" Johnny felt defensive.

"Thought I'd seen you in the area. Porter Square and Harvard. Brattle." The man shifted in place, exuding heavy smells.

"Never been there!" Johnny lied. It was getting easier.

"I saw your bags. The tags for Boston. There should be one for Cambridge. Without Cambridge the Bay State would sink into the Atlantic."

"I was just passing through. A tour." Johnny almost asked, "What are you doing here?" to turn the attention away from himself. But that would show an interest which could then lead to all sorts of attachments. "I don't expect to be back there."

"Name's Merve Rasker. Lived in Cambridge all my life and know every inch of it." The man stretched out a hand to Johnny. "Harvard '53. *Summa cum laude*."

Johnny mumbled his name.

"I didn't get it. Is it Frank?"

"Yah. Excuse me. I'm checking out." He was polite. Having lived thirteen years in the Boston area, almost a third of his life or even a little more, Johnny felt toward this stranger as toward a fellow citizen—*kababayan*—entitled to courtesy if not to outright attention. But he was not buying drinks or accepting any at the three bars of the Silahis.

"So am I, Frank. Maybe we can travel together...."

"Excuse me," Johnny fixed a smile on his face to cover his rage. He almost told the truth again: "I'm going home to my father." That would fix his location. But he didn't know the man's game. He could be from Immigration, Johnny thought, though he had caught Rick Fielder's squint in those eyes. Probably he'd spent a week on Mabini Street clutching all the young ass within sight, so he could winter with the memory back in Cambridge when thermal underwear and electric blankets failed to beat the cold.

"I thought...."

Johnny had a sixth sense about such things. It helped him stay away. Of course there was no reason Merve Rasker was not that and also Immigration—the way those guys bullied Filipinos in California, real *gestapo* stuff. Merve Rasker just might have his number, zeroing in on him, Juan in a million.

"Hold my bags," he told the desk clerk. Merve Rasker had moved out to stand at the front steps, either waiting for a taxi or for him. He was determined to outwait the man.

Bodies were starting to fill up the lobby, distracting Johnny, who avoided the front steps. Discovering the red public telephones, he decided to call his father and have someone to talk to until Merve Rasker disappeared.

The coin dropped. The phone's ringing disconnected Johnny from the lobby, from Merve Rasker. It sounded like an unearned name. Handed down. What if they had met at a conference, or sat on a panel or at a poetry reading at the Blacksmith House, or had listened to the string quartet at Passim's cardshop and restaurant, where he always got the hamburger done California style with lots of garlic?

No answer.

Suppose I flew back, he said to the receiver. He looked at his watch. Still time to get to the airport, March 5, and arrive—still March 5—after a flight of close to twenty-four hours. That time-frame again. The idea was tempting. Tuesday, he could be in his office to write the book for which he had gotten the sabbatical. He should have applied for a whole year at half salary, instead of just the spring term at full.

Closing circles was a compulsion with him. He just might pack up and go back. Well, he was already packed. All he needed to do was get a taxi to Manila International Airport, where Merve Rasker was also probably headed. But Johnny did not want to write that book for Rick Fielder. Magnetic fields and laser. What he should do was head for California where the newest laser labs were, then write his own book eventually. Fielder would never let him hear the end of it though, having already announced he had a publisher when he had none. "I'm letting John Manalo co-author, to help his promotion and tenure." Fielder was all heart, as big as a basketball.

Johnny looked to see where Merve Rasker had gone. Still out in front, a few yards back into the lobby. Waiting for whom?

The phone continued to ring. It felt as if his ear were attached to a tube focusing beams on a pellet of tritium. Someone picked up the receiver. Finally, finally. Hello? Yes? Hello?

The connection lasted those three questions. Either a woman's voice or that of a young boy, the sound twisted like a tongue.

The sun might have been a dead hawk in the sky. Johnny had trucked his bags to his father's house and here was a young man in *sando*, standing in his way and telling him to come back later.

"No one's home. The doctor left and he did not say anyone was coming today."

Perforated by light, the leaves formed a finely woven net to catch birds; yet the shadows were sharp and Johnny would not have been surprised to see a hanged man dangling from the tree.

Should he say he was the son, introduce himself to a stranger in the house where he grew up? The absurdity was just too great. The taxi had left and how was he to get another? Leave his bags there at the gate and walk to the Monument in the heat? It was getting more absurd. Every reason justified his leaving without a word, back to Boston.

Johnny's anger expanded to include his father, who certainly had flaws he had overlooked. For instance, his father never wrote to him, never asked him to come home.

He fumed inwardly, foul thoughts fortunately unspoken. As intense as the feelings he had about Rick Fielder for his escalating demands on Johnny's time and energy, rage and frustration merged with his disgust at meeting Merve Rasker in the lobby of the Silahis. Indeed they had met in Cambridge, indeed they both lived on Prentiss Street, opposite ends of it; and one Halloween, dressed in rented tuxedo, someone very like Merve Rasker had jumped out of the shadows behind a Darth Vader mask. Boo! Boo to you! Johnny merely walked on.

It was too dark to flash a smile: he justified his indifference. It could have been someone else, but he was sure it was Merve Rasker on the prowl before All Saints' Day. Did he, Johnny Manalo, have a scent attractive to the sexually ambiguous? Johnny Manalo, as usual mincing words, even unspoken words. There was no reason, except hypocrisy, to call them modern saints. That diminished sanctity.

Somehow, his thoughts must have registered on his face for the young man relented and opened the gate to him. "Perhaps, you can wait for the doctor inside." The young man even took the bags and carried them to the door.

He must have decided that he can grapple me to the ground if I turn out to be an intruder, Johnny thought somewhat ruefully. He took his time entering.

Immediately, Johnny felt good about his father again. Only Merve Rasker remained implanted in his anger. Why should the man have told him he came here every year? "In '80 I met the Lovely brothers. Turned out to be firebombers. Ineffectual though. Only succeeded in blowing off their own legs and arms." Johnny could not imagine Rasker recruiting for the opposition based in the States, or even smuggling out dollars or bringing in guns. Unlikely gunrunners were best at the job, though. People were not what they appeared to be. *Macho* males were mostly gay, the muscle was their cover.

"Are you the son from Boston?" The young man noticed the tags for Boston on his luggage.

Johnny barely nodded. The role of the son of the house forbade more than that.

"Coffee, *po*?"

"Is there beer?" Johnny asked, pulling out a magazine from the dusty pile under the coffee table. A woman in a swimsuit was on the cover. 1980.

"No, sir, but I can run to the store".

Now, he's trusting me with the entire house, Johnny thought with sarcasm, peeling off a couple of dollars for the beer. "Go ahead."

"I won't be long," the young man said, closing the door after himself.

A strange dog's bark came from somewhere. Another

unfriendly sound, Johnny thought, menaced by its reaching him inside his father's house. One step at a time he went upstairs. Martin's room was unlocked. A single bed, bare of sheets, stood in the middle of the waxed floor. A wardrobe with full-length mirror, a desk and two chairs completed the furnishings.

Johnny remembered it full of toys. Just above the floor, across from the door, there was a hole into which not a few marbles had disappeared, making the noise of traveling across the hidden length of the house inside the beams.

He also remembered himself and Martin standing on the sill above the clinic, hands holding onto the grilles and trying to see whose pee could arch farthest out into the garden, clearing the metal awning over the window below. The last feeble drops finally corroded the metal between their feet.

Johnny turned his back to the window and to the memories. He pulled the door noiselessly.

On the other side of the piano was his mother's room. He crossed under the gaze of St. Cecilia—was she not a saint who was beheaded?—and entered. Framed photographs, some as large as mirrors, hung from the walls. He did not remember them. What he recalled was his mother lying in bed, either reading the weekly *Liwayway* or just quietly with the rosary across her body, the way the beads lie on bodies inside caskets.

A vase of paper flowers held the cloth down on the round table where all kinds of candies used to be kept inside jars. He recalled the occasions when he had been in that room, listening to his father telling her what had happened at the clinic. Sometimes, at the end of his day, the doctor would bring up a handful of jasmine from the garden. He always kissed her on the forehead on entering and on leaving. The white mosquito net that used to billow over her bed when the windows were left open was in Johnny's thoughts. It reminded him of clouds over fields.

One of the bedcovers she crocheted now covered her bed. He expected to see her slippers side by side beneath, red embroidered slippers that made her feet look pale.

Once, his mother attempted to teach him and Martin to say the rosary. They took reluctant turns passing the rosary back and forth to each other. He remembered her gently holding the crucifix to their foreheads saying, "The cross is a real crossing. On it, the Lord came to us. On it, bearing our own sufferings, we go up to Him." He also remembered his father chiding her, "Don't tie my sons' hands with the rosary, they should be taught to rely upon themselves instead of being told that if God did not exist, it would not be possible to live."

Those words, forgotten meanwhile, came back with exactness, came with anger that she was dead and he had been left to believe with no clear object of belief.

He might have checked the wardrobe, to see if the quilted pink bedjacket from the Harvard Coop was hanging there. It was the only gift he had ever sent her. He had mailed it in brown wrapping paper for her birthday, the one year when he remembered it in time. But she didn't receive it. It took two months to arrive, and by that time she was dead.

He turned around, unable to walk forward by himself. In the room hung a photograph of her taller than she was in life. She was standing with a smile, a hand resting on a pedestal with books on it, the other holding a fan against her body. The thin transparent sleeves of her *saya*, the folded shawl of the same material, the overskirt almost rainlike with beads sewn in designs of flowers that were repeated in the serpentina skirt coiling down to her feet encased in white silk shoes—all this made it painful for him to watch her smile. He had never seen her walk. It could only have been at his birth that she was crippled.

The thought chased him from the door, down the stairs and out into the garden. Life was the beast from which no one was safe. He walked past flowers, thinking of the tiara in his mother's hair.

A dog barked again. It seemed to be the echo of his anger. Johnny decided to leave, to come back another time. Why could he not stand being home for any length of time?

Outside the gate, he felt ugly and powerless. Black exhaust blew from the tailpipes of passing buses that raced down the road, making it seem even narrower. He walked fast, eyes on the road.

"*Hijo*!" A car slowed down to a stop across from him.

As if they were forces of equal violence, Johnny's anger gave way to delight when he recognized his father. "I didn't know you still drove, Papá!"

"I started again after the last driver left. Get in."

His father pressed the horn outside the gate.

Johnny remember he had sent the young man for beer so he got out to open the gate himself, locking it after the car. "Where did you go?" he asked, opening the car door for his father.

"I came for you. The clerk said you had checked out. Remember I said we will have curry cooked the way your mother liked it? I picked up a pot of *kare* from the former maid. I hope Ismael boiled rice."

Johnny took the heavy pot from his father and followed him into the house. Without lingering downstairs, they headed for the kitchen where his father cleared space for the meal.

"Ismael forgot to start the rice," his father said and began to measure the grain into a clay pot.

Helpless, Johnny watched his father wash the rice. It felt awkward to have his father doing the work. "I'll send you a set of stainless steel pots," he offered.

"Rice has to be cooked in a clay pot, *hijo*."

Johnny made an attempt to clean the sink after his father had finished washing the rice. But when he saw a plateful of fishheads, the gills still bleeding, he sickened and walked away.

"Ismael will clean up, *hijo*. That's for the cats. There are a lot of strays. Once, you know, I found a dead one under your mother's bed. I don't know how it got into the house. At first I thought it was her slippers...."

"Come for a visit, Papá. You'll like Boston. You might even stay." He could see the two of them living on that boat in Boston Harbor, each one a lord to himself, like buddies.

"The pot will watch itself, *hijo*. Come into the *sala*."

They sat in front of the television set but did not turn it on. It would just be the President, his father explained; no use listening. "Lies," his father said. "I read the newspaper only to know which lies I should not believe."

Johnny repeated the invitation.

"Long ago, I would have said yes," his father answered, as if he had expected to be asked. "I know many things about New England. We were taught English and American literature and history, you know. When I can't sleep at night, Longfellow and Wordsworth come to me...*the murmuring pines and the hemlocks*. Once I wanted to see Walden Pond, Emerson's home, the Alcotts'. All those people...but now I'm too old to travel. When I could, your mother...I would not have left her alone. I've met all the people I want to meet and seen everything I am supposed to see, *hijo*."

"Too old, Papá? No way! My landlady is 90. She takes the subway to Boston and lunches at the Parker House. She figures out her own taxes and reads the business section of the newspaper before she turns to the comics. News is the last page she reads."

"My ears are still good, though." His father got up to check the rice. "The pot is boiling hard. I should have lowered the flames. I can read the newspaper without glasses. But my legs are going. And my hands. I lost my grip two years ago.''

Johnny smiled but could not suppress a yawn.

''Take Martin's room while you're here. Bring your bags up. You know, it takes time to get over jet lag. It takes longer than it does for planes, for the body to cross the time zones.''

The bed was made when he returned upstairs.

''It's not bad being home, is it?'' his father held the door open for him.

''No,'' Johnny answered, not certain if that was the truth or just another lie. He undressed facing the wall and missed the fighting cocks, missed the phone that would ring only for him. Did Sylvia Mendez know the number at his father's house? At that very moment was she thinking of him in any terms? And what about Rose Quarter? Was she counting the days to April Fool's? There was mixed urgency to the answers he wanted.

The bedding smelled of soap, harsh soap that cleaned and nothing more. He had missed that raw smell when he first got to the States. It went with firecrackers and crickets at night, with rice cakes cooked blue in bamboo tubes, smothered with sugar and freshly grated coconut....

Chance or deliberate act, it did not matter what had brought him back; although, falling asleep, Johnny knew that home was also another space 8,000 miles away. In his sleep he broke free and floated his way back there; back to isolators and spatial filters, helium nuclei and elements that could mimic each other's reactions.

The loud knocking matched the pain in Johnny's dream of a white flower sprouting inside his ear. He was trying to wrench it out but both his arms were held at his side while the rippling spiral of the flower's roots took over his body. The more he struggled, the deeper the roots went. The flower even grew sharp edges, glass that drew blood.

"Wake up. Wake up." His father was bending over him.

When the sound became words capable of delivering their message, Johnny broke clear of the dream. Sitting up, he felt the surge of blood inside his head. Who was he? The question begged an answer he could not give, uncomfortable as he was with himself, even in sleep.

"Come." His father was standing beside his bed, wearing white that reminded Johnny of the metal bed in the clinic, of the white sheet and the jars of formaldehyde.... "Will you drive, *hijo*? I can't at night. My eyes."

"What day is it?" Johnny asked, lost in his dream wanderings.

"You slept all day. It's Tuesday night."

Johnny slipped into his trousers, buttoned his shirt as he stepped into his shoes. Walking down the stairs with his belt still unbuckled, he felt as if things were blowing through the house, a storm rushing. He ran both hands through his hair, wishing he could shower first.

A man he did not recognize was standing at the foot of the stairs, a woven hat, like a too-large emblem, held in his hands. Though he wore what looked like church clothes, he had on rubber slippers. Johnny remembered that his father never demanded that poor patients leave their slippers at the door and enter on their bare feet, as his mother wanted.

"Ismael, close up after us," Johnny's father called to the young man who had let Johnny into the house the day before.

Johnny got into the car, turned on the engine and gunned it down, not knowing how fast it would catch since he had not driven it before.

"Clear on this side," his father guided him. "I think I should have this driveway paved and widened. Another meter should do." The long leaves of the oleander touched the sides of the car. "Okay on this side, *hijo*. Just take care of yours."

Eyes on the rearview mirror—he had flunked his first test for a license in Massachusetts because no one had warned him he should look back over the seat and not use the mirror—Johnny backed out of the garage, thinking of the time he had sat in the back with his father learning to drive. Used to the driver closing the car door after him, his father had backed out and slammed the open door loose against the *duhat* tree. He could see it coming but he could not call out. Watching from the house, his mother had dropped her beads. The fallen rosary, Salud told him, formed the outline of a cat.

The man was holding the gate open on Johnny's side while Ismael held its other half out of the way. As the car drew closer, the taillights lit up both men's bodies until for an instant they appeared to have emerged suddenly. Once past the gate, the headlights picked out both men's faces, their arms held against the glare.

"Rio's father," Johnny's father explained. "He came to let me know that Rio has been found beside the bridge, on the other side of the fishponds. With another body. A neighbor of theirs."

"Dead?" Johnny could not believe what he heard. It was too farfetched a result of his sending the boy for the taxi.

"Where is the boy now?" Johnny's father asked the man who had gotten into the back seat.

"At the house when I left. We can't afford a funeral parlor, Doctor. Anyway, the nearest one is up in town, too far away."

"There is Father Armand's chapel."

"Yes, Doctor."

"Well?"

"My wife says no. Because he's not ordained, Doctor."

"I know. But anyone can see from looking at him that

he's saintly. This man really wants to be a priest, *hijo*. It just so happened he could not pass the seminary courses. And look, Macario. God has always worked with the most unlikely people. Look at Peter and the others. Fishermen. Luke was a doctor, of course. But look at his prophets. Gideon was the most insignificant of an insignificant family. The trouble is, in our wisdom, what we consider our wisdom, we think we can choose better prophets and priests than God can.''

The turn of the conversation amused Johnny. Real grace through a priest who had ordained himself. It was pure sentiment. Arbitrary kindness or blindness. If the laws of physics were laid down in that manner there would be no stability....

"*Hijo*! Down *El Heroes del 96*. Cut across Samson and to the left. Macario, this is my son. The one from the States. Rio saw him. The first day Johnny came. Just go on. Keep going, *hijo*.''

"What happened to Rio?" Johnny asked Macario, who bent forward respectfully as if the fact of Johnny's visit had taken precedence over his child's death.

"We can't tell. A neighbor found the two bodies. Perhaps some secret marshals were having fun when the two came along. The minute I heard people coming to the house, my heart turned. As if it knew already. The same fear came immediately to my wife.''

One corner after another followed, not at right angles or equal distances as they did in the States. The doctor called them out as they approached and Johnny recognized a few after they passed. He remembered that the land sloped down into the fishponds outside the town they were entering.

"Are we headed for Libis?" Johnny asked.

"Beyond," his father answered.

"Just outside Libis," Macario added. "Right on top of the garbage dump we pick for a living. I used to be a fisherman but Japanese trawlers drag our waters now. Before that I worked in a pineapple plantation. We got open sores because we were given no protective clothing while we sprayed the fruits. There's a sardine factory near here, but too many are on the waiting list...."

Stay on your right, *hijo*," his father cautioned. "Macario is one of the I don't know how many million squatters here, *hijo*. Actually, I figured it out one day, out of cartons and crates you squatters have built more houses than the government. The official funds do not even cover those earning below 300 pesos a month. They may cover housing for the very rich and loans for hotels, even hotels being built in China, but not for those who really need housing."

Johnny stopped listening; the conversation did not interest him.

"Our need just makes the government mad. At our other settlement, without warning, in full battle gear the soldiers came to move us. Those who resisted got hit by assault rifles and 'pillbox' explosives. The soldiers would not allow us to salvage part of our huts and in the new place, where we are now, it rained and rained. The small and weak caught pneumonia. Several infants died. No water, no electricity, no food. The next time we're chased out, I'm thinking of living under a bridge...."

"I don't understand," the doctor said, "this New Society is supposed to be a compassionate society, but all it seems interested in doing is to make the poor disappear instead of helping them. *Balik probinsya* is Madame's latest: 'squatter councils'—for squatter-control. Then there is the anti-squatting task force. The same money could be put into housing for farmers displaced by agri-business, fishermen pushed out by foreign trawlers."

It was too dark for Johnny to see anything but the road. The headlights picked up every stone on the trail. During the rainy season, he imagined there would be no path at all, just mud.

The car creaked. The shift was not working too well. Each time they hit a hole it felt as if the car would fall apart.

But like the furtive end of a tunnel, light appeared out of the darkness. And an odor as of dead bodies. Macario suggested that Johnny park away from the freshly dumped garbage or they might blow a tire.

"Let's walk the rest of the way," his father said. "Park about here, Macario?"

"Yes, Doctor."

"Is that not the chapel?" The doctor asked. "There seem to be a lot of people there."

"I can't believe it," Macario said. "She brought Rio to the chapel after all. When I suggested it, she asked me, 'Can God be there if the priest is not a real priest?' I can't believe it."

Johnny saw an unfinished structure with a makeshift altar in the middle of the floor. A crucifix, man-high, stood with some statues away from the walls, which were partly covered with fresh masonry. There was a representation of the Holy Trinity: God the Father was exactly like God the Son, except that the statue had white hair. The Holy Spirit was a dove whose wings rested upon the haloes, joining them. The three might have been carved out of a single piece. There was an Immaculate Conception, and another statue of the Virgin standing on a globe.

Macario walked directly to the small coffin set on wooden trestles used by the workmen. Six candles were burning on the floor, their light too far down to reach the basket of calla lilies that had begun to wither.

Johnny approached behind his father and looked down into the coffin. Remorse did not come since he knew nothing particular about Rio.

"He was a good son," Rio's mother came to them, stood

with much longing on her face beside the coffin. "Each time he came, he gave me what you pay him, Doctor. 'Use it, *Inay*. What's left keep for my shoes.' The last time he was in a hurry, I had to call him back so I could bless him before he left again. He had never come that late before. Said something about a taxi. I must have misheard him...."

Johnny wanted to speak to the woman as he passed her on the way outside, but nothing came to him. More than anything he wanted to be out of that place, be in some spot where he could breathe, with Sylvia Mendez and the smell of flowers on her arms, instead of with the smell of refuse.

Mourners stood outside under the tree or just inside the threshold. Women came in holding on to each other's hands as they looked at Rio. The odor came from their hands and their hair.

"He worried about us," Rio's mother told them. "As young as he was, he was thoughtful. One day he said to me, a neighbor told him foreigners gave him and his sister money and clothes. 'Just let them do something to you and they'll give you money, too.' At least he died untouched."

"Things like this force people to cling to the sharp edge of the blade," Johnny's father said, making way for other mourners.

More women came, bringing tears to each other's eyes. The men stood at some distance, watching without looking-in their direction.

"He is at peace now," the doctor stopped again to comfort Rio's mother before leaving. "Where he is now, shoes are no longer important."

"He also wanted to taste an apple," Rio's mother broke away from the women's hands. "Doctor, he would ask me, 'What does an apple taste like, *Inay*?' He was only eight. This Christmas I wanted to surprise him with an apple....."

"There are apple trees in Paradise." A man in a white

cassock came over with a smile full of innocence so that, although he was in his sixties, he looked like a boy himself.

There are apple trees in Paradise. Johnny felt his eyes fill at the artlessness of the thought, without guile but also full of hope.

"Shall we pray for Rio now?" Father Armand asked, calling them all together with his hand. " 'Wherever two or three are gathered in my name, there I am in their midst.' What gospel story shall we start with? How about the prodigal son or the woman who touched the hem of Jesus' garment? You remember that Jesus felt the power going out of His body. He looked around and said, 'Someone touched me.' His disciples answered, 'How can anyone find out who?' You remember that there were so many people. A big crowd had gathered, waiting to be healed. As there are so many here. But Jesus knows when we touch him. And how do we touch Jesus? We pray. Even if we say just one word. Even if we just think that word: God. Here in this book, it says a woman touched Jesus' garment and she got well. Let's see what was wrong with her."

Johnny watched Father Armand look among the pages for the passage, so rapt in his search, so fixed in his concentration that Johnny's curiosity passed into attention and he pressed closer to hear the words as they came out of Father Armand's mouth. "In Paradise we will live as long as God..."

Able to hear only her own grief, Rio's mother moaned, "Rio, Rio. *Anák*, why did they take you from me? Sixty stab wounds. Not even his bones were spared. Only a butcher can do that. Slice even the bone. *Anák, anák*. Your mother is crying...." And she fell against the pew, the weight of her body pulling down the women clutching her hands.

"Don't say anything more. We know it, too," the women whispered, trying to ease her pain.

But she sat up straight and shouted. "If only his father did not act so boldly. If he had just remained quiet. It did not help anyway. But every time we are evicted...that man I married twenty-one years ago, it was Christmas, the day of the King of Peace.... He told the soldiers, 'You have no right. We are human beings. Not eyesores, not what your Madame calls economic saboteurs....' " Her voice lost its edge, became softly plaintive, a song not set to music. "...not human refuse or criminals...."

"It's not Macario's fault," the doctor said. "No one here is to blame."

"Whose fault is it, Doctor?" the woman asked without looking up. "If God had only listened. I try not to ask too many things in my prayers. I made the sign of the cross on Rio's forehead as he left. '*Anák*, be careful,' I said. I wanted him to stay for the night and return to the doctor's house the next morning.... When Pidiong died, Rio was only a toddler. Pidiong was killed, too...when we were being relocated the first time. He wanted to save something from our hut, a book, I think. He grabbed it, then ran. I never knew if he felt the bullet. It went through the back of his head and there he was....Macario and I lifted him up to the truck. He was already dead.... The soldiers were hurrying us and Pidiong was heavy. 'Your turn will come,' someone cursed the soldiers, shouting. It was Macario."

Father Armand had now read the story of the centurion and was asking them to say the *Our Father* a second time. Afterward, reading from an old and tattered book of *English Rituals*, an aspergillum in the other hand, he began sprinkling holy water on the coffin. Large drops fell about it on the floor. It appeared to be a ritual washing, a baptism, by a priest practising vows he imposed upon himself.

"And for us," Father Armand turned around to sprinkle the mourners. Some knelt as his hand lifted over them. Some remained standing or seated. Johnny felt the drops in his hair, on his neck, soft heavy drops that sent a shiver through his body.

"It's in the Scripture," Father Armand said. "It's in God's Holy Bible that we will receive our dead back through resurrection."

Once more Father Armand opened the holy book, started reading. In his hurry and his excitement, he read like a schoolboy skipping words to get to the end.

"The same things Rio had when he was baptized—candle, white cloth, water—are what we have today for him. He has been cleansed from sin, from selfishness, which is at the root of all sin. We are cleansed along with him. That's in Scripture, too. The word of God, the Word which became Jesus."

Rio's mother sat back, sagging against the pew. Her eyes closed. Her breathing rose and fell.

The sprinkling drew the people deeper into the chapel. Some had never set foot inside. Some called it the Church of the Squatters. Father Armand himself called it the Holy and Immaculate Conception of the Catholic and Apostolic Church of the Holy Trinity.

"Something has come to me," Rio's mother said, trying to stand up. "Let me tell my son."

The women would not allow her to rise, to pull out of their grasp. Fear of what they did not know made them restrain her.

"Let me, let me," she said, using force to free herself. "Let me."

"Leave trouble alone," they answered. "Rio is an angel in heaven now. Father Armand said there are apple trees in Paradise." They used the very words they had laughed at when Father Armand said them.

"I'll tell you anyway," she shouted, lifting her head above the women struggling to hold her down and quiet. "It's the government. It's that Madame and Marcos. They killed Aquino, too. They send out death squads after anyone they please. Rio was killed because his father was in that protest march to Malacañang. I'm not afraid. I know there are informers in this place. Let them hear...."

Macario broke through the women's bodies to reach his wife. "Please forgive her. She does not know what she's saying." He tried to lift her up, to carry her away.

"I won't leave my son," she protested, "Let me stay. I won't say anything any more—not even the truth."

"These are friends," he said, his arms still about her. "They know how we feel. We don't have to tell them what's in our hearts." At this point, tears came to his own eyes and he walked out of the chapel.

As soon as she was free of his arms, she said, "Sixty stab wounds. Such a small body. We sent him to live with the doctor so he could be safe. Here, suddenly the police and the soldiers come looking for someone. Paid to kill, the syndicates come. Before words are spoken, guns burst....Then they come to haul us off to another place, worse than before. Where the earth is too hard for seeds to grow...."

"Forget it," the women said, returning to their places surrounding her. "Forget it for Rio's sake."

That only goaded her. "Do you know what will happen next?" she asked the women wiping her face and neck with the ends of her shawl. "The next time it will be to the cemetery they'll haul us off. See what happened to Ariston!"

"Not now. Someday we'll talk about all these things. But not now. Father Armand is praying."

"Ariston disappeared because he bragged in front of Ines' *tienda* that he knew of the videotape that's supposed to be missing—the one showing soldiers shooting Aquino. He was delivering something to this general's house and the driver and servants were talking about it...."

"Enough. Your husband said so. God knows. He is listening to our hearts and when the time comes, God will do something."

"It will be too late for Rio," she sobbed. "It might come

for some but not for my son." She wiped her face with her shawl, sobbed louder into it. The cloth could not muffle her cry. "And too late for Aling Angge's son. Didn't the soldiers refuse to pay for the beer they drank? Didn't they spray the store with their guns, striking every bottle on the shelves and hitting their own lieutenant, a new PMA graduate, in the back and legs when he tried to stop them? It's too late for all of them."

Johnny moved back, out of the chapel into the clearing in front. Father Armand could be heard reading another lesson, like someone making a first-time discovery. Out under the acacia a current of air moved, parting the leaves. A few stars were in the sky. There, his father came to him.

"We can go, *hijo*," his father said. "I left an offering for both of us."

"It is I who should have given," Johnny said, about to admit that he had set in motion the chain of events that ended in Rio dead.

"Why you?"

His answer stopped in Johnny's throat like matter that had abruptly immaterialized. Through his body passed the sound of Rio's mother crying: Come, Lord Jesus, come quickly.

"*Pare*," a friend followed Macario outside as he accompanied Johnny and his father to the car. "*Pare*, there's a way to find out who killed Rio. The faith healer."

"I'll go with you, afterward. Wait."

"Maybe the doctor and his son would like to see how it works," the man stepped toward the car. "I have seen it work, Doctor. It doesn't fail."

"Why not?" Johnny answered for both of them.

They walked deeper into the squatter area, stepping into soft ground that, in the dark, seemed to Johnny to have been brought up from the earth. The faithhealer's house was a *barong-barong* with a car tire to hold down the makeshift roof.

"He worked in the electronics factory till his lungs were burned by the fumes from open vats of chemicals. I'm lucky to be unemployed. Our neighbor got sick at the same factory and was laid off. Ended up jobless anyway—and sick. Jobless is good enough for me. Now and then the garbage yields something. It's good enough."

The faith healer came out of the single room where his children and wife slept on two mats, sharing the space with jute sacks filled with plastic bags and metal scraps they had scavenged from the garbage heaps. As if he had been expecting them, without being asked he brought out a basin of water and a used candle.

"That candle is from the church in town. He's a sacristan there on Sunday. He will not go into Father Armand's chapel."

They followed the faith healer to the side of the house built from crates and cardboard. A puppy was asleep inside a box lined with rags. It whined to be petted as they passed.

At the back, the faith healer guided them with the candle held toward the ground so they could see where they were stepping. Mosquitoes flew in pairs where they stopped to stand around the basin set on the ground. The flame fluttered like a moth lifting its wings before sinking in the water.

"He accepts neither gifts nor money," Macario's friend told them, whispering. "You can beg him and force him, he will still refuse. He says his powers will be taken from him if he accepts. And he is better than the faith-healers who get rich from the foreigners."

"Yes. Without knowing it, he happened to bathe in a stream after an angel had washed itself there, and his body absorbed mysterious healing powers, a gift to see things clearly. Don't you believe in these things?"

"How will he do it?"

"Watch. He will hold the candle above the water in the basin. Slowly, as he prays, a face will appear...."

"An actual face?" Johnny asked, biting off further comment. Just in case, he looked down from the hand that held the candle with much shaking so that the flame sputtered on the water where its wax bled.

Trying to start fresh without bad memories, Johnny Manalo went to see Sylvia Mendez as soon as he could get away from his father the next morning. It was Wednesday, March 7. He felt as if he had never left home.

In expectation that the *Lakbayan* march to protest Aquino's death would soon reach the Monument area, traffic was heavy. Johnny decided to fill the tank of his father's car while waiting for the traffic to ease.

The station attendant handed him a flyer about the Central Luzon Freedom Marchers who had been in Meycauayan the night before. According to the flyer about 15,000 camped, joined by thousands of citizens, children of political detainees, homeless poor, various organizations until 30,000—not just those who started out from Malolos ten thousand strong—were met by the town with food and water. The priest and mayor of Meycauayan greeted those who had stopped midway at Marilao.

Gas cost easily three times more here than in the States and this discovery annoyed Johnny. He threw the flyer on the seat beside him, and waited for a break in the flow of traffic to get out of the gas station onto the highway.

The sense of urgency he felt came out of his impatience, not his feelings.

Sylvia Mendez was still asleep, the maid said. Unaware of marchers and the brash stirrings of Johnny's heart. He sat out in the veranda where Sylvia's self-appointed campaign workers had waited hours while he and Sylvia raced under the light rail posts from one end of the city to the other.

Orange juice with ice cubes was brought out to him, and a cloth napkin into which was woven a white design of trees. He watched the ice dilute the juice, drumming his fingers on the arm of the wrought-iron chair that matched the table topped with glass. No reason for his coming occurred to him, besides wanting to see Sylvia. Made to wait, his thoughts circled, closed in on Rio laid out in the wooden coffin as thin as the balsa wood of assembly-kit models, on the freedom marchers out in the sun. Did life consist only of violation and violence? Life, Mary Brewer said, was not for the weakhearted.

Unable to think of an excuse for coming, Johnny prepared for an exchange of hostilities, as if they were already lovers who had to arouse themselves through the infliction of pain.

"Johnny Manalo!" Sylvia Mendez came out in a long gown that had not been slept in. "Calling in the middle of the day! Is that Stateside custom?"

"You must run, you know. The ticket needs you. Also..." His voice dropped as he was telling her to run for the sake of Rio. It was not what he had planned, or wanted to say.

"Another Pete Alvarez! I'm overwhelmed. But I've already decided, Johnny. No. NO! Why should I? The opposition can't make up its mind whether to urge people to vote or to boycott, and I am expected to make up my mind? Actually, I had decided yes, until I saw you."

There was nothing he could say. The professed object of his visit had been rejected. Without another word, without another glance in her direction, Johnny stood up to leave. With absolute clarity, his mind saw the design on the tiles on the way down, saw the sunlight falling sharply on the stones of the walk creating a path in the middle of the garden.

"Wait. Johnny Manalo. Come back. I didn't mean it that

way. You're too thin-skinned for a Stateside Filipino." She was running after him on soft pink slippers. The sky joined the blue of her gown when she leaned back slightly against the car door to keep him there. They might have been standing there unseen under moonlight with the wind carrying the scent of hidden flowers. All the sounds, except that of Johnny's heart, had stopped.

What was he to say?

The next instant she was leaning toward him, slipping an arm through his, leading him back up the stairs onto the veranda whose tiles had become waves rushing the shore.

A maid bringing out two glasses of orange juice for them, on seeing them arm in arm, dropped her eyes, turned about, back into the house, her face as tight as a cat's paw.

Sylvia laughed. "You shocked her, Johnny Manalo. Coming unannounced and...really! Sit down across from me and let's talk properly in case she comes out again."

He reached for the glass of juice on the glass-topped table to ease his throat but she reached over to hold his hand.

"That's all water now. Don't. She'll bring new drinks out after she recovers." She laughed again, but weakly this time.

A sip was all he wanted and he took it.

"Did you come only to ask me to run for the Batasan? I didn't mean to compare you with Pete. I was teasing. I thought you could take jokes. Pete is good. Nice to have around. Except, once he starts talking, and anything can set him off.... Is it important to you that I run, Johnny? And who is this Rio? Did she make you come to tell me what to do?"

He was back in her power to do with as she pleased, was never really free from it—a fact they both knew as they sat there.

"Rio was a boy who died."

"So I should run for the Batasan?" She got up to sit closer. "Boys die every day, Johnny."

"He disappeared and was found dead—sixty stab wounds. His father is one of the squatters' leaders. At least he joins protests."

She pulled out a sigh, held it, then crossed her legs the other way. Checking her nails, she finally replied. "Walter does not think that I should, with no chance against a candidate of the President. I think I can win. But so what? That's not what I want to do. This isn't the States, Johnny. It's a cockfight here. Double spurs. There will be smear campaigns, a whole sordid scenario will be made up just for me. The Black Madonna.... No thank you!"

"A boy died. Nothing! Boys die every day. It does not even make good poetry." The intensity behind his words surprised Johnny. It sounded as if somebody else had spoken.

The maid brought out the glasses once more.

"I'll tell you what, Johnny. I have an appointment I can't wriggle out of today. But...will you save one day for us? Say Friday? You're not leaving that soon, are you? Save the whole day. Twenty-four hours. All twenty-four. So we can do something terrific that will make you come back." She smiled, lifted a glass to her lips. Though she barely drank, her mouth looked smeared. "I'm late. Dreadfully. I'll have to say someone dropped in without warning. That will be the excuse. Stayed and stayed."

Was she teasing again?

He stood up almost as soon as she did, had just steadied himself when she came over to throw her arms about him, without touching him with her body; then was gone—as if the two acts were one—walking quickly into the house, almost running.

Rather than wait, not knowing if Sylvia Mendez was coming out again or not until Friday, Johnny Manalo showed himself to the gate before a chauffeur or maid could come out to dismiss him. He used the word dismiss intentionally, the way someone else might clench a fist around a cigarette butt to feel pain. Half-heartedly, he tried to think of Rose Quarter but she was too far away to be claimed at random.

Though he did not want to, in case someone was watching from the house, Johnny turned to look back in an effort to piece together what Sylvia had said. He was on a very short leash if he came back Friday, he thought, beheading the flowers that bloomed beside the gate. The flowerheads were still in his hand when he heard himself being called.

"Johnny!" Sylvia Mendez was coming down, running breathlessly. Why would she take leave of him on the veranda only to come out again in the same gown? It was beyond him. When she stood between him and her shadow on the grass, he felt he had been pushed fast forward to Friday. Was it Friday already in her mind?

He, who needed to know reasons and the cause of things, felt uneasy. If she had intended that he follow her into her bedroom, she should have said so. Too long in the States, he needed things said outright, no mistaken intents. He needed to see grooves and pegs matching. But nothing Sylvia said or did seemed to have any source in herself. Was she on drugs? Or on a steady fix of attention, for which she would attempt anything?

He thought of his friend Steve, who was so afraid for his health that he wouldn't even take headache pills. Afraid his heart would give out, he never took a woman to bed. His wife was always being found under the bushes during picnics, with men he did not know.

"Johnny, those are *mimosas*," Sylvia pointed to flowers by the gate, averting her eyes from those clutched in his hand.

His father had the same flowers in pots. "I know," he said, recognizing the ones he had pulled off.

"You know flowers? That's a surprise." She walked into the garden, toward a vine that had wound itself on a wooden wheel set on top of a pole. Its branches dragged in the wind. "I'm beginning to like you, Johnny Manalo. Do you know why?" She pulled some orange flowers, beheading them as Johnny had done. "Because you treat me the way a brother would. Other men want to marry me. Like Martin. They think that gives them the right to bed a woman. So they end up married to several. Life is unreal, Johnny. Most people are."

Another farfetched idea, Johnny thought, intrigued.

"There were three of us, all girls. Leticia used to play under that tree with dolls almost as tall as she. I hated dolls."

"What did you play with, then?"

"I never played. What I liked was for the maids to roll out a mat underneath the trees whose fruits had ripened, then to have them shake the tree and make the fruits fall. Leticia did not like being stained with the dark juices. I liked that on my hair and face. I had short fat legs then. I bounced," she said, lifting her hem partway up. "Then there was Clara. Some kind of neuralgic disorder made her seem retarded, to walk awkwardly; but she was regal when she merely stood still. You'd think she was a queen." She moved on again.

Where Johnny caught up with her, she stopped and turned abruptly.

"Clara read a lot. She could pick up languages the way Leticia picked up men friends." Sylvia stopped, waited for his face to react.

When he said nothing and stood there without flinching she went on.

"Clara wanted to see Constantinople. Do you know why, Johnny?"

"I can't guess."

"Well...." she said, walking on again.

He stepped where she had stepped, wondering what other ciful tale she would tell. Were her thoughts only connected by chance? Or was everything ultimately relevant so that no matter what was said or in what order, it was true and at once fact; the way time differed in the separate zones of the world but really coincided; the way the light of dead stars reached the earth millions of years after they were gone, but for all intents and purposes existed still. That thought contained for him a glimmer of eternity, of endlessness and time without beginning. Natural but confusing, the way he wanted to hold her, to crush her and also to leave right then and never come back. Hang Friday! He stood there, waiting to listen to what he could not see the point of, to what she could not be keeping track of in her mind.

Side by side they reached a fountain that spouted greenish water, shuddering in the sunlight. It seemed to be the garden's exhalation.

"She wanted to see Mary and Joseph's house."

Of course. Prepared to be surprised, still he was caught off guard. "Wasn't that in Bethlehem or Jerusalem?" he managed to ask. The Holy Land somewhere?

Eliptical shadows fell upon the fountain.

"Angels lifted the house to Constantinople, didn't you know? And then, again to save it, lifted it up to Loreto. That's where Clara saw it."

So Clara got to Loreto. "Where is she now?"

Sylvia walked around the fountain, and halfway from him, stopped to answer, not his question but the one in her mind. "Clara married a Frenchman...thirty years older. Maybe he was older than he appeared to be. He had this big stone house outside Paris. I don't recall in what direction. A huge thing with practically no kitchen, only huge beautiful rooms with chairs that looked as if they were posing. Clara's description. He spoke only French. She sent picture Instead of children or furniture, she had pots of flower plants all over the house, some you could not put your a around."

"Quite interesting," he said.

"Occasionally, she called. She acquired this lovely accent. Why not come and visit? she always asked. Then one morning, at two or three—since then I wake up each night at the same time—a call came through from Paris, or the place outside Paris where they lived...I can't recall the name. It was he calling. She had just died." She looked up at the sky, then down on the grass before slowly walking her way back to him. "He wanted to know if he could bury her there, if we would insist on having her body...."

He dared not ask what was decided.

That was part of what she wanted to tell him. "Leticia was somewhere I couldn't reach. I called back. I said I would attend the funeral. It was lovely. All 135 people who lived in the village were in church. Not a seat left. I was late. The plane was delayed or I couldn't get a car right away. I stood just inside the door throughout. I followed to the cemetery. Walking, you know, trying to remember everything I could about Clara. Then it was over. I got back in the car. I had not introduced myself. I did not want...I couldn't. She looked so pale, so thin and fine. It was her. And also a photograph. A photograph laid to rest. A lovely one. I cried on the way back. The chauffeur I had hired kept on saying, Madame, Madame.... I had suddenly grown old. I felt very heavy and old. Inside the car, passing people in the country who stopped to look at me, I felt I was inside a coffin. It was November. I had a coat but my fingers froze and I thought of Clara cold in the ground. Do you like this fountain?"

The fountain was a broken bird of some kind, possibly a crane.

"It broke apart when Manila was being liberated from the Japanese. Imagine the beak and a fish going head first with the water coming out of the tail fin. Papá was a lawyer. He died when I was three. He was very tall. At night he either read or worked on his stamp collection. Nineteenth-century stamps. While he worked he could listen to the fountain. Edges are very important with stamps.''

He knew. He had begun a stamp collection but found it made him restless cutting the glassine covers to fit. And he was never sure what kind of stamps to collect.

"Mamá did not cry when he died. She went to her room and locked herself in. Three days later, after Papá had been waked and buried, she came out to move us all out of the house. I bought back the house. Rather, Walter did. It's exactly the way it was before. Some of the furniture I recovered.... The people did not want to sell. The house was lucky for them, they said....'' She was facing the house, her lips shaping words she had stopped speaking.

Johnny followed her eyes. Birds were flying in and out of the eaves. His seatmate on the plane had said he'd heard there were no birds in Manila any more. "Only flies, I was told.''

"Look at the saplings, Johnny. They're moving closer and closer to the house. In no time at all their branches will sweep the windows.'' She turned. "They're like the trees where Clara lived in France, marching toward the house. You know, I think she and her husband lived for each other....'' Sylvia started walking away.

By the time he caught up with her, she had finished what she was saying.

Grass grew in patches under the larger trees whose roots lengthened close to the ground, making it impossible to dig-in plants, so these were grown in pots. A tree had fallen, bringing down part of the fence which had been repaired with different-sized stones.

Clearly, it was that house that was important to her, that house and the memories it held for her of the lives she wanted to persist, past deaths and dying. He wondered if

100

she had ever walked with Martin in that garden, or with Pete Alvarez.

For some time, without speaking they stood against shrubs of pink and red hibiscus growing into each other, forming a hollow for them.

"Decide for me, Johnny. Should I run?"

It tore his heart to hear her ask. In self-protection he warned himself that all her sweetness could be hiding a gross center, but he could not make himself believe that.

On the way to Puerto Azul with Martin, overcoming his tendency to assume that whatever happened took place according to some mysterious natural order, Johnny wondered how his brother had tracked him to Sylvia Mendez.

Instead of answering the question he posed, Martin pulled an envelope from his shirt pocket. "Take a look. I brought this to the hotel for you but the clerk said you had checked out, had gone to the airport. I called Papá. How can you stand Papá? He doesn't talk, for one thing. He doesn't want to do anything." This did not explain how he had come to look for him at Sylvia's.

"Who are they?" Johnny peered at the photograph inside the envelope.

"That's us when we were kids. The smaller one is me." Martin took a hand from the wheel to point to himself. "I found it inside a book. How it got there, I don't know. That's Salud between us. You remember Salud, don't you?"

The picture made Johnny's heart sink. If Martin was the smaller, then it had to be he who was born in the clinic. Johnny pressed a thumbnail into the smiles, tearing all three faces before returning the envelope to his pocket. At least, it could have been their mother between them, instead of Salud.

"I meant to send that to you in the States, but I didn't know your address."

"I don't think I should go to Puerto Azul today. Papa does not know and he'll wait for me. Sometime next week...."

"He knows. I even asked him if he wanted to come. It's a party for one of Leticia's boys and she asked me to bring you. Walter also asked for you. It will be different fun."

They stopped for drinks at the InterCon as if there was no hurry. Johnny hoped Sylvia Mendez would happen to pass by.

"First-class bitch, that Sylvia Mendez," Martin tossed in the statement with no warning. "Walter convinced our people to run her for the Batasan. It took a lot of favors and then she decided to run on the opposition ticket. If I were Walter...."

"Walter?" Johnny asked, fishing for information different from Sylvia's.

"Leticia's better half. He has this thing about Leticia. He suspects everyone. He'll even think you and Leticia will have mated. That's his term. Once he acquires proof, he relaxes and looks for the next person to suspect. He can't have children and he wants children. Handsome children, no less. So he has no choice."

"But will he be at Puerto Azul?"

"No. He can't travel. Since he was shot by their security guard. In a fit of jealousy he challenged the guard to a duel. Then, shot in the spine, he refused to have the guard fired. He's mental. He wants the children around him all the time, but they can only remind him.... Didn't you notice? No two look alike."

Martin was taking no precaution not to be overheard and Johnny was becoming uneasy.

"Do you know why Walter always has a lighter though he doesn't smoke? When Leticia threatens to leave, he can threaten to set fire to himself. Poor Walter. He just looks and touches. Can you imagine that? Just touches, man! Leticia told me. She's a real saint."

Johnny toyed with the idea of telling his brother what Sylvia had confided about Leticia's emotional divorces, but he was anxious to be somewhere else. Besides, how could he tell his brother that Sylvia said he was Walter's pimp; that his wife Aida was supported in the States by allowing property of top officials to be registered in her name. He refused another drink.

"In that case, let's go. I'll just pick up a gift for Leticia." Martin called for the bill and flashed his gold credit card. "We'll cross to Fe Panlilio, I'll get Leticia a trinket."

There was a security guard in front and another just inside the door of the jewelry shop. As soon as Martin was recognized, the door swung open. Martin walked quickly down the display cases.

"Wrap that one up," Martin said to the salesgirl, who had the hauteur of top fashion models.

At the official exchange rate, the necklace of blue sapphires cost easily twenty thousand dollars. Other prices in that store were even higher.

Outside, Martin gestured casually with the long thin box with narrow ribbons. "Quite a place. When it's busy you'll meet Arabs and U.N. Officials here".

Stepping out of the way of young boys being chauffeured around the stores, Johnny thought of Rio who wanted to know what an apple tastes like, of Pete Alvarez talking as if his life revolved around squatters and the urban poor.

Martin eased the car out of the tight space in one turn. "I can tell that Sylvia Mendez has knocked you out. Stay away from her, Johnny. Her brain is all screwed up. She's man-crazy. Right now young activists give her a high. She wants Walter, too. And me. Don't think I'm making this up."

What an imagination his brother had. That was not the

Sylvia Mendez he knew. Johnny slid down in the passenger seat, closed his eyes to concentrate on reasons why Martin would be explicating her sins. Transgressions make a good mouthful.

"You're not going to fall asleep on me, are you?"

Johnny pretended to be asleep. Watching the scenery through slightly-parted lids took his mind off what Martin was saying.

A large part of the trip on the South Super Highway was along Laguna de Bay, whose shoreline was edged with factories. He saw smokestacks thickening the air, saw the spires of an Iglesia ni Cristo like a large tombstone beside a Roman Catholic church, fields and hills of housing. Above the Bay, the sky was the color of oystershells. He recalled an item in the first newspaper he had bought on the way to Dewey Boulevard: Fishermen floating dead on Laguna de Bay, casualties of a feud—fishermen against military and other officials who had sectioned off the communal bayshore as their private fishponds. How like the turn-of-the-century tenancy feuds under the Spanish regime—an echo of Rizal's novels.

What about martial law would the national hero have written had he lived nowadays? The martial law administrators, improving on the Spaniards, would have had Rizal shot as he stepped off the boat, instead of waiting to arrest him and execute him at Luneta.

Johnny wondered how the bullet felt in the instant of death. Occasionally he had attended political meetings in Cambridge, but he always stayed in the background. He heard Charito Planas speak at St. Paul's. Once a priest from Negros spoke about the oppression of the *sacadas* working in the sugar plantations. There was Manglapus' Movement for Free Philippines, a moderate group. And he knew Phil Suva Martin, chairman of the Boston chapter.

Loaded with vegetables, jeepneys snarled the traffic.

"Tourist, tell me if you want to stop anywhere," Martin offered. "How about some *espasol* or *puto seco*? Something you can't get Stateside. Before you leave I'll take you to Pansol. There's a club there I was interested in. Solviento. Luckily I learned in time that it's heavily mortgaged and the Development Bank is anxious to unload it. I'll look at it one more time, then decide."

Johnny sat upright. He had seen bananas in stalks and looked back at the long row of wayside stalls on both sides of the road. There was something reassuring in their presence, in the calm way the vendors looked out at the road, just observing, with no hurry and no expectation, it seemed.

"Did you see the banana stalks?" Martin braked, then throwing the gear in reverse, backed up on the two-lane road. "The birthday boy might get a kick out of that. Think of it, Johnny. If you could have all the bananas you could care to eat...what kind would you like?"

Johnny helped lay the bananas on the back seat in order to keep them intact. And Martin drove with less speed; but when they arrived at Puerto Azul after two hours, the fruits had dropped into random piles that reminded Johnny of the huge slugs in the redwood forests of Woodside, California—the exact size of the yellow *señoritas* that had fallen off their stems.

"Shit!" Martin cursed. "Throw them out," he called to a workman who was sweeping leaves from the parking lot.

Laying his broom on the ground, the man lifted the fruits carefully into his hat. Running out of room, he improvised a basket out of his shirt taking much too long for Martin, who was anxious to look for the birthday party.

Moved by the care with which the man handled the bananas, Johnny reached into the back seat for the rest and received the man's gratitude, for Martin had walked ahead.

"Hurry," Martin called.

Johnny locked the car, stepped quickly toward the sea, a blue flicker of wings in the distance.

"Nothing for the birthday boy then," Martin sulked. "Do you have anything? How about some dollars? That might amuse him. Teach him to save for the next trip abroad."

Johnny took out his wallet and Martin started to count.

"I'll write you a check for this from my dollar account. Nice and crisp. Thanks." Martin flipped the bills over. "I think the kids at the pool are Leticia's. Come on."

Only the children and their *yayas* were there.

"Wow," the birthday boy took the wad of $100 bills in his wet hands and passed it around to the others who tried to recognize Franklin's face on the bills. One bright boy calculated the peso value, "Times twenty. Sixteen thou."

"That will buy only a small stone," a little girl in a hot pink swimsuit said, more interested in the signature on the other side.

Soon enough the excitement faded. The children began diving to surface at the other end. A *yaya* leaned over to pick up the bills floating in the pool.

"They might have appreciated the bananas more," Johnny thought, still thinking of the bills in the water as his. How would he remind his brother to pay up? He watched the *yaya* place the bills under a pair of imported sandals. Just like play money, he thought.

"*Tito*," the birthday boy pulled away from the others to come up over the edge, hanging on to the gutter. "Thank you for coming to my party."

The remark took Johnny out of his thoughts and he dropped down to where the boy was clinging. "My pleasure", he said. "I didn't know it was your birthday. I would have brought a gift." He was thinking of the stuffed giraffes, half-grown or full-size at Calliope on Brattle Street.

"Anything at all?"

"Depends." Johnny was on his guard against the eight-

106

year-old.

"How about a book with words, all words all over. This thick and with the alphabet?"

"A dictionary?" The simple request surprised Johnny and endeared the boy to him. He had expected someone spoiled to ask for the moon. Or a comet complete with tail. So he lifted the boy out of the water to hold him up high as a treat.

"Put me down. Put me back in the water." The boy struggled with his whole body. "It will be your fault if I catch a cold, *Tito*. My mother will get mad at you."

Johnny got wet from his thrashing, angered by the boy's quick turn of temper. From the snickering and the rippling reflections of the sun, he headed towards the clubhouse.

"Don't forget, *Tito*. Don't forget about the dictionary. The biggest one. I want to go to Harvard and be smart. Did you go to Harvard, Tito?"

As a matter of fact, I went to MIT. Johnny thought of turning around to inform the boy who had disappeared into the children turning somersaults in the deep end of the pool, unceremoniously breaking off the conversation with patriarchal ease.

Johnny tracked sand into the clubhouse, where he saw Sylvia Mendez and Pete Alvarez in an alcove. Her hair, again, was a mass of curls. In a sundress, unaided by wire cups, her breasts were small.

"Hi!" Pete said, getting up before Johnny could walk away.

Hands in his pockets, Johnny walked over reluctantly. Pete's presence so fractured the moment that the lobby appeared to be a darkened passageway. A short distance from the alcove, he stopped, forcing them to come to him. It was not fair for Pete Alvarez to make a battleground of Sylvia.

"Hello," Sylvia Mendez said as she brushed away Pete's hand on her shoulder. But she seemed to walk past Johnny.

His confidence shattered, Johnny was certain all the advantages would be Pete's, if people looking down from the mezzanine were comparing them. Yet Sylvia Mendez was obviously older than Pete. Pete could be her child, Johnny thought bitterly.

So after all there was nothing to that walk earlier in her garden when she had confided not a few lives to him. But obligations were based on reciprocity and he had confided nothing in return. He felt like someone full of passions that led nowhere but deeper into himself, and this thought made him angry. An old man at 38. He had not, before this, considered himself old. In chino pants and Nike sneakers, he felt impervious to aging; the way hard wood repelled moisture.

Coming in burned by the sun or going out greasy with sunblocks, people pushed them together or cut between them mercifully. Making way for others took the place of a conversation no one cared to begin.

"There you are," Leticia cried out on seeing them bunched up. "Huts all arranged. Hurry and take your pick." She was holding Martin's arm wihout shyness, animating him with her lightheartedness. "Every hut has a view of the sea. Isn't that marvellous? Seabreeze at night. And no mosquitoes. I hope." She acted as if she and Johnny had greeted each other before. "Come, Johnny."

Johnny wondered if the smile would drop from her mouth if he asked about Walter. Or would she merely, and glibly, tell him another version of Walter, entirely different from Martin's and Sylvia Mendez'?

But she did not wait for him. She was waving to the children in the pool, having broken away from Martin to walk hand in hand with her sister, forcing Pete to back off from Sylvia. The sisters looked like small girls on the way to a fantasy, though Johnny could overhear the tone of argument in which Sylvia was saying, "Walter said I could bring anyone I want."

The reference was to Pete, Johnny assumed. He figured that Alvarez could want several things from Sylvia.

"Walter's resting right now," Leticia said, stopping at one of the huts and letting go of Sylvia's hand.

Raised wooden passageways connected a group of huts above whose roofs, shaped like Moro *vintas*, Johnny saw the branches of trees he could not name. He felt powerfully singled out by Leticia's explanation and he stopped, in case more was forthcoming.

Still, Johnny could not have seen the woman through the window of the hut more than an instant. Naturally he looked away at once, his mind playing back what he saw, imagining the rest: the woman straddled atop Walter, her entire length either giving him warmth or taking his; her mouth still open, her body about to lift up from crouching. Johnny was certain that, together, the two bodies emitted a sound.

"Who was that?" Johnny hurried after Martin on the passageway walled with plants startling in the color of their flowers and the shape of their foliage.

"I'll see you at supper," Martin said, brushing off his question and entering the next hut.

Johnny was not prepared for this abruptness. Alvarez' coming could not be the whole reason why no one was friendly any more, even his brother. Should he have seen it coming from the pointless artifice with which Sylvia and Leticia had decorated their laughter with facial grimaces, teenagers mugging for the camera, then running from each other suddenly? What was Martin's confession all about, his saying he envied Johnny's simpler life, the absence of obsessions—"You're right, Johnny. Life is not all hustling" —since now he would not give Johnny the time of day.

Could it be a faith healer on top of Walter?

Johnny wondered which hut was still empty, thinking vaguely of a turtle he had seen climbing out of the Charles River with a great chunk of its shell gone, leaving it open for predators to tear into its flesh. Was that the way he was to these people, made vulnerable by his candor, by his tendency to accept what they said at face value?

"Johnny!" Sylvia was calling from one of the huts. "Hi!" Her voice was barely raised above a whisper.

He had been so shunned and courted by quick turns since he arrived that Johnny stopped guessing which it was going to be this time. "Hi!" he replied with a minimum of enthusiasm. Through the window he saw a bed covered with white sailcloth and the hastily scattered contents of suitcases. He moved on, past buds of bird-of-paradise flowers, purple-crested, orange-throated above the railings of the passageway.

"Are we neighbors?" she called after him.

"No. Johnny is down at the last hut," Martin answered from inside his own. "Johnny, shut your door so they will know it is occupied."

Johnny let his brother's answer speak for him, taking on the indifference of someone just passing through. It was wrong to expect the dazzle of permanent stars when all that grew there were trees with fruits as dark as bats.

"Aren't we?" she insisted, as if this was her central concern. Something unspeakable and wild in her asking taunted him.

He entered his hut although he wanted to stay out on the passageway where Sylvia Mendez could call to him. As soon as he shut the door, he heard the sea, the sound of someone trying to enter. Though very tired, he walked out again but right down to the shore. Thin clouds were riding above the sun. He expected a barricade of sorts, restrictions, notice of limitations as on many beaches in the States. The clear stretch of sand unnerved him.

What could that beach have been once, he wondered, watching the sea gathering white against the sand. And what would he remember of that moment? This coarse wind or his standing outside her door, compelled and restrained by the same force? He did not know what to insist upon. In three weeks, or less, he would be gone.

One shock after another, waves ran aground on the sand. He imagined voices opposing each other. What were his obligations, having been willed into flesh in some unremembered place and forsaken time? Some salt-soaked beach so distant that it left no trace in the memory. Out of fairness to all involved, it should be possible to acquire a sense of destiny outside of a family, outside of a country and its history.

Merged with others, would he become free of involuntary memories and be able to expel that child born in the clinic from his thoughts? Following the shore, he walked close to the trees, seeking solace. He sensed a flutter overhead. At first it appeared to be a heavy leaf turning from its weight, but after staring hard, he discovered it to be a bird caught in a web. Its struggle was perfectly contained. Overcoming his shock, Johnny looked about for a branch with which to tear apart the web and free the bird, for a stone to hurl at the mesh of spun filament.

A hand upon his shoulder failed to startle him, so caught up was he with the struggling bird.

"Yes, it's heartless," Leticia said, looking up and then quickly away. Her hand was on his shoulder, seeking comfort.

There was no sound anywhere, just some music playing with no beginning and no end.

"It will free itself soon enough," Johnny said, though he doubted this. He led Leticia away so she could be startled instead by flowers. Once shared, the dread he felt could no longer make him yield to fright.

She resisted being led back toward the huts but brought him to a place she knew, leading with her hand lightly. There was still a view of the sea, up a slope of shrubs with the heavy trunks of wide-crowned trees.

"Look," they said to each other as the sky was seen to dip into the sea.

She leaned against him with the pressure of softly scented laughter, bringing them to forget the struggle inside the web. Not pristine, but as close to innocence as hearts could incite each other, they accepted the cover of clouds and weeping trees. Staining the grass before rising hand in hand, they then headed back separately.

Awkwardly, Johnny wondered if this was love. What had just happened seemed to have rooted his soul to his body, though it was not Leticia he wanted. The next instant he felt unheroic, someone who had simply masturbated in someone else's body.

"Walter?" Leticia spoke quietly, her voice hard, her hands held below her breasts, when Johnny Manalo sought her out in the dining room before taking his place at supper. "Walter has nothing at all to do with what I do. If you must know, Johnny, you might as well learn it from me. Walter's...He's...he's castrated. All he has is a hole, just like a woman. Don't tell me you're shocked."

With that remark, she took her own seat, smiling so that the others could suppose they had exchanged some ordinary pleasantry. Then seeing him still standing, unsure of what else to expect, she indicated his seat with the hand he had held earlier. She then looked down the table and across to catch the drifting of her guests' attention.

She might have said, to teach Johnny a lesson: Yesterday never happened and tomorrow is today. Nothing is real if I don't say so.

Leticia's words and smile spun a web about Johnny, but he managed to take his seat. Completely crushed by the rasp of her voice—all softness and grace gone—questions came one after another to disturb him. What she had said, partly confirming Martin, explained everything, yet nothing. What about that woman he had seen so intimate with Walter? And what about the mistresses on separate floors? What about Sylvia, his brother, himself?

Johnny let his eyes wander outside where the sun was bleeding into the sky, burning itself out as it set. Why was he here? To amuse Leticia and her sister; to roll over on command like a pet?

If Martin knew about the slope of shrubs with its view toward the sea, he did not ramble lost in the discussions. Johnny watched him and the super-executives from Makati dissect the economy on the tablecloth, predicting which banks would close, which investment firms would stop paying dividends due to the slump.

At the other end of the table an American historian studying on a Japanese foundation grant was arguing that the Japanese never intended to occupy the Philippines, but only wanted to push ahead to the negotiating table. Someone else remembered that the Japanese had bombed Manila after it was declared an open city, remembered the waves and waves of occupying forces, and broke in, "Unplanned or not, three years of torture, of looting the country to feed Japan, of finally seeing people drop from hunger in the streets—these were unmitigated...."

Johnny turned his plate around. This had nothing to do with him. Sylvia Mendez had not appeared. Neither had Pete Alvarez. He felt disowned, ignored by Leticia and Martin.

Across the table from him, two men were discussing how many faithful, meditating in the world, could bring about peace. They leaned across to introduce themselves, professors from the University of the Unified Field. Well-dressed media-types, they told him that 1984 was a crucial year for their movement. From the Philippines as a place of psychic healing, they intended to spread their enlightenment principles to the rest of Southeast Asia. "The Maharishi," the Canadian said, "was much encouraged by the President's reception...."

Johnny was watching the children at the other table being made much of by waiters and by their *yayas*, who were cutting their meat and deboning their fish, holding the pieces patiently on poised forks until the children opened their mouths. He did not see Sylvia Mendez arrive.

She took one of the empty seats with no explanation for being late. Soup had been served. Johnny dared not look in her direction for fear she knew, had been told, had seen him and Leticia, so he turned toward the man who was saying how transcendental meditation had improved his sex life. "TM makes an entirely different person out of you. You are put in control, able to deal powerfully with others, with situations. That surge of power connects you to everyone and everything. With the cosmos. Antagonisms cease...."

"Prayers also do that," someone from the marriage encounter movement said. "Deep personal prayers connect you not just to the cosmos but to God. It is well to remember Paul's Letter to the Colossians. See to it that no one deceives you through any empty, seductive philosophy that follows mere human traditions, a philosophy based on cosmic powers rather than on Christ...."

"But prayers keep you tense on your knees while TM relaxes you."

"Is relaxation the purpose of life?..."

"Please," Leticia pleaded. "Nothing serious or deep. It hinders digestion...."

"Excuse me," a man three seats down called to Johnny. "Do you know where Boston College is?"

Johnny nodded.

"I earned pocket money at the dining room of St. Mary's. Used to have lobster on Fridays. There was a priest who had been to the Culion leper colony; he had glass slides of Intramuros. The process is quite expensive....I wonder if he's willing to donate the slides to a museum here. If I remember right, his name was Father Meagher."

Martin called from his end of the table, "Johnny can find out for you, I'm sure. He and the Jesuits have something, at least one thing, in common. Clean living. Sheltered, safe life. He'll outlive us all, like that old priest."

The conceit took the words out of Johnny's mouth. Like the memory of a fire, it fixed in his mind what Leticia had said about Walter, the bird's struggle inside the web, and his own surge smearing the grass where he and Leticia had briefly lain.

Johnny simply stood up and without a word walked away. It was exactly how those people would have acted, and the thought lightened his steps, made him feel incomparable like them; but not for long. He soon missed the ear-shattering dissonance at Leticia's table.

A few *yayas*, collecting mosquito bites outside, made way for him. "Good night, sir," they said together.

He groaned a reply.

It was pitch black away from the lamp posts. He remembered that night came about the same time every season. The realization told him, more than seeing his father had, that he was home. To stay?

There were whispers from the direction of the beach so he walked away, backtracking to his hut. With the persistence of crickets, the whispers whirred inside his ears. Or perhaps they were crickets with the sibilance of whispers. In any case, could they be commanded to silence? His annoyance amplified the noise, gave it undertones.

115

High enough to allow a grown man to walk beneath, his raised hut reminded him: someone had been brought to his father's clinic, slashed through the gaps in his bamboo floor. Assailant unknown.

A change of clothes had been hung in the closet which had been left open. He showered, then made an effort to sleep. Was it still Thursday?

He woke up and fell asleep again. Woke up and calculated it was still Thursday. He had not lost a sun's rising or setting. But without his watch he felt lost; he had left it at his father's house.

At three a.m. or so he sat up. Having slept a couple of hours, he was ready for the day. He had forgotten about the whispers. Was someone else awake? Sylvia perhaps. Or perhaps the guest who was raising money for paraplegics and to whom Johnny had made a pledge just before Martin informed him this was a con-man, collecting on behalf of groups who never saw a peso afterwards.

He got up to peer through the slats. Puerto Azul was emotionally far from anything he knew, so that he felt physically distant from everything as well. He played back whatever he could recall happening since he arrived, trying to get a fix on where he was. The poor people of Macario, Pete Alvarez, the rich cronies carting off millions in government funds to invest in foreign nest eggs—these had nothing to do with him. Nothing depended upon what he thought, said or did. He was an absolutely free man.

Unstructured situations unsettled him. He wished he knew what was planned for the day, what to anticipate or avoid.

He did five minutes of exercises on the floor beside the bed, but his muscles were all bunched up and he hurt. He looked for a pad to write a letter, a Bible to fall asleep with again—motels and hotels in the States always had one in each room, courtesy of the Gideons. Then he heard the waves. But there was no way of knowing whom he might run into, so he stayed put.

Light had not broken through the clouds and he decided he had a couple more hours to sleep. Toward daybreak, he had a dream in which, on all fours, he was digging his way to the other side of the earth, coming out in Revere, north of Boston. Or was it Paragon Park in Nantasket? The dream only fixed his sense of dislocation.

Gentle reminiscence alternated with frantic efforts, still within his dream, during which he would find himself drifting like a lily pad or thrown at the sky, aloft with huts flying, large pieces of roofs inverting the heavens, fire spinning and tumbling. Through all that he felt the absence of his father.

Awakened by that sense of loss, he got out of bed, showered, changed into the clothes left for him, someone else's, and hurried to the dining room to catch up with the party at breakfast. It was almost time for lunch; no one was there, no trace of anyone. It felt as if nothing had continued from the day before.

When he asked, he was served breakfast anyway: a slice of papaya, coffee, a plate of *longoniza* and scrambled eggs that tasted different—organic maybe. Laid by hens that scratched the earth, unfumigated by pesticides, unfed by hormones to speed up growth.

Johnny lingered, waiting for someone to come out for a late breakfast or lunch. He asked for another cup of coffee. Instead of refilling his cup, a fresh one was brought steaming hot to him. He was offered a newspaper but he refused it.

Far off, a *banca* with outriggers was hanging on to the waves. Watching the boat's struggle brought his thoughts back to himself. Was it the beginning of madness to wonder who he was; from time to time to have to stop and wonder?

"What kind of fish is caught out there?" he called a waiter over to distract him from his thoughts.

The waiter did not know. "I'm from Manila, sir."

117

Johnny kept the boat within his sight, a permanent shadow. "A bay as large as that and probably not on any map," he remarked.

"Yes, sir," the waiter said, smiling.

"It seems so," Johnny said, wanting badly to have someone to exchange a word with, any word.

Another cup of coffee and he felt compelled to push off, out into the sun, which sculpted every surface around, repeating its shape in complete or partial form over the landscape. He used to catch his students' attention first off, by telling them to bring thumb and forefinger together, then let the sunlight through. Whatever shape the fingers made, the sun would make a perfect circle on the wall or ground. As it falls through space, he would then tell them, light repeated the sun's circularity.

What did it mean, this, in terms of human desire, for example? In terms of his father and his wish to be with him either there or in his father's own house? In terms of Rose Quarter? And Sylvia Mendez most of all?

Johnny stepped out in the direction of the water, heading for some answers. As he came closer, the shore seemed to open up, incised with light and fire; and his thoughts pushed off against the waves that were coming from great distances to meet him.

Johnny Manalo was beginning to recover himself, stepping back into the long walks he used to take through unnamed coves up at Rockport and into Maine—a man alone, naming everything he saw—when he heard his own name being called.

"Johnny!"

Unrecognizable in the distance, as if the face was deformed by a hood of nylon stocking, a man was waving for him to come. Johnny stood his ground, forcing the other to come to him.

"Johnny!" Out of breath running, Martin looked as if someone had just died. "Something happened. Can you help?"

The agitated rhythm of his brother's breathing updated the torn picture in Johnny's wallet. "What?"

"Pete Alvarez was shot. In Sylvia's car on the way to Hidden Valley to give the children a different swimming hole...."

Relieved that nothing had happened to his father, yet still upset that he had been left behind, either deliberately or as an oversight, Johnny could ask no further questions.

"Leticia and the rest were far ahead, luckily. I was the only one following Sylvia's car when it happened. I heard a shot. Like a motor backfiring, but I saw her car going off the road. I parked alongside and her driver came to me saying, 'I shot Mr. Alvarez.' I understood at once." Saying those words in sequence calmed Martin down and he was able to smile.

"You took Alvarez to the hospital and called the police?"

A cloud passed over both of them, its shadow separating them on the sands of Puerto Azul.

"No," Martin's smile tightened. "He was dead. What would be the use?" The next instant, face-saving gestures over, Martin added, "You're right. But the driver is prepared to admit that he shot Alvarez."

"Then he didn't?" Johnny asked, recalling Martin's story about Leticia's eldest boy shooting someone in the men's room and Walter's driver owning up to the crime and going to jail for it. "Didn't he?" Johnny became suspicious. "Who was driving?"

"Of course, the driver," Martin answered quickly, resentful of his brother's prying. But as if to cover up his doubts, he explained, "I remembered you were back here, so I returned. I'm sure everything is settled by now. Nothing to worry about."

"What did Sylvia say?" Questions began asking themselves in Johnny's mind. "Didn't she try to stop it?" Was it really an oversight that he had been left back at Puerto Azul? Walter was supposed to have been asking to meet him. Where was Walter?

"Look, Johnny, this is not Stateside. No one will ask those questions."

"There has to be a reason, Martin." Johnny felt like an upstart brother trying to bring the other to his knees. Some passion must have impelled the shooting. Whose? In the absence of answers, Johnny tried to re-enact the incident in his mind. Was someone being protected? Or was he only being dramatic instead of trying to close the gaps he saw in the narration?

"Let's forget it. I just had to get it off my chest. I told the driver to dump the body behind the trees, then take Sylvia on to Hidden Valley. Not to stop till he got there and not to tell any one. He can be trusted. Come on. They're waiting for us. It's still a birthday party. Leticia wants it to last as long as possible. Let's go."

"And Walter wants to meet me?" Johnny asked sarcastically, not expecting an answer. He followed Martin to the parking lot, trying to be calm so the right answers would come to him. He felt out of phase with himself, like a pulse of light whipping about an oscillator. Something did not sound right; either withheld or stated out of sequence.

It felt airless inside the car though outside he could see the wind whipping the aerial.

"Was it robbery?" The question posed itself, separate from Johnny's will.

"Stop conducting an investigation, Inspector. Drop it." Johnny decided to concentrate instead on some mental exercise that would work unconsciously on the problem; anything that would set off the series of inferences that would add up, having fueled the inquiry in the right direction.

He began imagining the nuclei of hydrogen atoms releasing energy at temperatures greater than the heat at the center of suns. Was *destroy* the same as *create* in some dictionary?

The length of the road, ahead of them and behind, large passenger buses belched out dark exhaust that thickened the air. The shadow of trees moved across the road as they followed its winding.

Sullen and depressed, Johnny considered another possibility. Suppose Martin had done it? And was going to use him as a fall guy! More questions along the same line confided themselves to him but he restrained himself from asking.

Corn was boiling in petroleum cans along the road, smoke marking the roadside stands. Trees he did not recognize grew between rows of coconut palms. Dusty vines linked trees branch to branch.

If it was robbery.... A mountain came up on their right but he was still too resentful to ask for its name. In the States there would be a sign nearby; markers give you the names of rivers you are crossing, even if they are no wider that creeks.

Johnny slid lower in his seat, closed his eyes. Nothing he was seeing mattered or changed things for him. Bright blue laser tubes alternated in his mind with shots being fired. Where was Pete Alvarez wounded? How many times? Did the bullet/bullets come out or lodge inside his body? From what angle did they enter? His mind spread out to spatial filters and isolators and beams emerging, the width of human hair, yet thousands of times brighter than sunlight seen by the unaided eye. The sun's circularity. Suddenly changing orbits....

"About here was where it happened." Martin slowed down.

Johnny sat up, his eyes skimming the tops of grass.

"Do you want to get out and look?"

Johnny did not, but did. As on the plane, one knee was fusing from sitting too long in one position. His back ached halfway up his spine, shooting pains to his shoulders.

It did not look like a place where anyone had been killed. Johnny walked about, taking short steps. Had the blood dried? Whorls of grass made him think of the fur on cattle. A few more steps and there was an incline. He walked toward it, then returned to the car. He did not want to see the body.

Martin went up ahead, pulling himself on the lengths of grass that cut his hands so that suddenly he let go to lick them, and almost lost his balance. For some time he stood there, looking down before returning to the car.

"Did the car go out of control when the shot was fired?" Johnny asked, finally relenting.

"I didn't notice."

Johnny's thoughts now focused on Sylvia Mendez. Why should he suspect her when she had no more motive than the driver? Suppose it had been Sylvia who had been shot, would he take the time to devise questions? The death saddened him though Alvarez meant little to him. Everything that had happened so far could easily become past and recoverable—except the killing. He felt implicated. And if Sylvia Mendez....

How could he walk on another beach without thinking of that day when Martin called to him on the beach of Puerto Azul? Stones glinting with mica in the sand would only make him think of messages left for some distant walker to decode or to throw back to the waves which would bring them to some other shore: messages about Pete Alvarez, about Rio....

He needed to rethink his life drastically. And he had just begun to become convinced it was possible to come home to stay, to start over again.

122

Suppose a fatal error had been made that would betray them all later. Someone who had heard the shots and saw....

"Let's forget it," Martin said, overtaking another bus.

"If you died, would you have any regrets?" Johnny asked. What was it that Pete had wanted to know and now would never?

"How should I know?" Martin answered. Some questions were not worth asking. "Forget it."

"Is Sylvia in shock?" Johnny asked his question another way.

"I suppose. But she is tough. She's a black widow. When she tires of lovers.... One time at a party—she likes the young kids—one of her boyfriends was found dead in the bedroom. No killer to be found. Investigation concluded it was a suicide. Just so Sylvia could not come to lay flowers on his grave, the boy's parents moved the body secretly...."

The road went up, skirting a rise of coconut trees—this was no untamed forest. If Pete Alvarez had been dumped down some hidden slope....but maybe he was not supposed to remain hidden forever....Only until it no longer mattered....

Johnny did not protest Martin's description of Sylvia Mendez. What Martin said were lies, without his being a liar necessarily. Johnny turned the subject over and over, baiting his mind. Finally, to rid himself of further questions, he offered to drive.

But Martin gripped the steering wheel, pushing the accelerator to the floor. The shadows of trees fell away from them, making them emerge and fade in a swift succession of thrusts that made Johnny feel he and everything else had blurred.

Birds of many colors in small rattan cages were being offered for sale near the entrance to Hidden Valley. Johnny Manalo wondered how the birds could last, their wings as good as clipped. Were he younger and filled with noble ideas, he would have stopped to buy all the birds in order to set them free.

The birthday party was in full swing beside one of the natural pools fed by springs. *Yayas* sat ready with towels, forming a curious assortment that reminded Johnny of nuns he once saw at the pergola overlooking Wright Park in Baguio.

He ambled along behind Martin, taking in the forest of *lanzones* trees. If he had come in November he would have seen fruits clustered on the branches. Salud told them a story about why the surface of the fruits had the mark of finger-prints. The Virgin Mary had touched the once-poisonous fruits so the hungry people could eat them.

"*Tito, Tito!*" Water dripped from the birthday boy's hair as he surfaced to call to them.

Johnny felt strange being called *Tito* instead of *Tio*. Perhaps the old title for uncle was reserved for blood relations. Children knew what parents were up to. Once, flying back from Florida, he sat across the aisle from a little girl who was talking to her doll during the entire trip. It was her travelling companion:

"Parker is my real Dad, Trisha. John is my stepdad. When Parker and my Mommy, I mean my Daddy and my Mommy got 'vorced, Mommy married John, so he's my second Dad. Aunt Libby said, we'll be with John and Mommy a week so I can meet the new baby. So Trisha, remember. Be polite."

On and on the explanation went, except while the meal was being served, when the little girl pretended to be asleep. On and on afterward, she was still trying to understand what she was explaining to her doll.

There was something sad in common between that little girl with her pink cotton blouse, white dirndl, sandals and frilly anklets, her hair in pink and white ribbons, and halfway across the globe, the spoiled boy whose father had only a hole, just like a woman, and how many *Titos*?

Martin entered the cottage before which Leticia's car was parked. Johnny took off down a path hidden by trees rising like many folds of the sky, thinking, for want of anything else, about the boat he had planned to live in, anchored off the Constitution Hill Marina. Ocean-going cottage.

Johnny did not expect to go all the way down the path. When he caught sight of Leticia puffing her cigarette, wearing white shorts and a pink blouse with blue and green stripes—barefoot she reached only up to Martin's ear— Johnny expected to be asked to come in, too, to be called as he walked away. Where was her sister?

He had no choice but to keep on going, now thinking of Fielder, who kept getting more grants on the basis of previous grants he had not deserved. The domino theory applied to everything.

No choice but to keep on. A fine mist, such as he had seen in Pennsylvania mountains, appeared to crown the trees, making them seem the original of those early American paintings of wilderness tamed by rainbows.

If nothing else happened to him on his visit, was being in Hidden Valley a good enough reason to have come home? He came upon a small pool. Pebble-locked. A few leaves floated on the dark surface that glistened like wet shells. Insects walked upon it without rippling the water. He picked up a stone with which to disturb, to agitate the pool, but threw it against a tree instead.

Everywhere there were *lanzones* trees, crowns tight and branching narrow. Living in such a place might beat living in a boat. A natural hermitage. Along the ridges of mountains at the edge of the Valley of the Fallen outside Madrid, there were stone hermitages, piles of rocks really. Inside the forest of Buaçao in northern Portugal there was a monastery which was then a summer palace before eventually it was turned into a hotel. The sky hung from the trees.

Another pool stood in his way.

So much was he inside himself that thoughts of Rose Quarter and Sylvia Mendez did not intrude. He ran his hand across the bark of trees, as if to leave his scent on them, claiming what he saw. Birds dropped down through the leaves to the lower branches that rested on the shrubs. A mockingbird, he recalled, always flew up to the tallest tree, singing the songs of other birds. Cardinals he had seen flying upward branch by branch on the white birches, their song short metallic clicks.

A trail of children crossed his path further up. Barefoot and sun-darkened children who hurried away when he called to give them some coins.

Their running touched something spontaneous in Johnny Manalo and he followed them, hurrying into a clearing where the land began to slope toward a river. The clarity of the sky, repeated in the air and in the water leaping past rocks below—facts to which in isolation he would have remained indifferent—gave him a sense of coming face to face with unprotected innocence.

It could be that he always envied children playing, a man and a woman walking abreast, or sitting in a restaurant or park with eyes only for each other.

Johnny watched the children stepping from rock to rock, hands held out for balance or holding on to the shoulders ahead, linking laughter when someone slipped into the stream flowing around boulders, forming rivulets that carried the shadow of the clouds to the cave on the other bank, over the children and their laughter.

If only his father were there; there in his place if not beside him. He felt the answer to his questions lay in being where the grass crossed and re-crossed the paths that rose and dropped according to some inconstant pattern.

126

When and if the four forces in nature were proven to conform to a single unified pattern—in a lab in Cambridge scientists waited to observe a proton disintegrate, destroy itself in obedience to an existing model that would hold true for all matter—would human emotions ever be found in parallel conformity?

Johnny felt the presence of something fierce about to overrun everything within sight; and he, unwilling witness, could only watch, helpless and unfaithful.

Before Johnny could process more unearthly propositions to counter the quickly-changing moment, Martin called to him.

"Let's go before it gets dark."

Johnny remained where he stood, staring down at the river, at the children crossing it toward a cave, which sunlight appeared to penetrate its length.

"There's nothing there. Let's go."

His brother's indifference just when he had spotted the children's destination and he himself wanted to go down to see how deep the cave went, felt to Johnny like a live bullet in his heart. He had been tricked. All along, proud of his wariness in following the children, he was the one being tracked unawares.

Raw-nerved, he shot back an answer which was all sound, a foul spatter of the anger he felt at being summoned when he was not ready. Who was Martin anyway but someone who lost and gained by mere handfuls, small of vision and with oddly parcelled dreams—Sylvia Mendez' own words! Except out of envy, why should his brother, just as he was about to grasp what was within him, want to call him away?

Yet, frightened by his anger at being pulled any which way without his assent and at the convenience of others, resentful and sullen, Johnny came up anyway. But not toward Martin, who had to cross over to him.

"She said, 'Drop it. Walter will take care of everything. You saw nothing, Martin. Forget it.' And Leticia would not let me see her sister." Martin overtook Johnny.

"Was it Sylvia Mendez who shot Alvarez?" Johnny asked the last thing he knew his brother expected or wanted to hear. The expression on Martin's face confirmed nothing for Johnny. Sylvia Mendez had been right; Martin did not have the imagination or the guts to want the power that went with being rich. Somehow, he thought of his brother in terms of the blue jay fledgling he had found pushed out of its nest one rainy spring. He found it crumpled in the grass and nestled it in an old towel, drop-fed it sugared water and bits of meat; still, having become hollow inside, the food came out of it as fast as it entered: a little bird quaking with cold, trying to chirp until finally, after three days, no longer able to hold its head upright, it fell over, claws tightly curled, feathers dull and rent.

"How can I forget?" Martin asked, standing there suddenly like someone with no clothes on.

The helplessness in his brother's asking foreclosed any further pursuit. It felt to Johnny that the real sun was in another sky, rambling.

It was more or less unbroken silence between them during the break-neck four or five hours back to Manila. Deliberately, Johnny did not ask his brother to come into their father's house when he got out at the gate. He did not even turn around to wave.

Dim lights linked the windows of the house. Johnny rang the bell only after Martin had sped away. Standing at the gate, waiting, he recalled it was only a week ago that he had arrived. Yet it seemed that he had never left. And that he had no other place to go.

"Have you had supper?" his father asked, opening the gate himself. Already clad in pyjamas, he looked like a man proud of not having more than he needed.

The question reassembled Johnny's thoughts. Something in the way his father stood made Johnny think of the photograph Martin had given him on Wednesday. It lay where he had jammed it into his pocket, crumpled like a handerkerchief.

Johnny Manalo watched his father pour rice into the clay pot, turn on the faucet and let the water run until the grains swirled loose and fast. After putting the pot on the stove and covering it, his father dipped a hand once more into the pot to check the water's height. He seemed as serious as someone measuring the future.

With the same care, his father cut tomatoes, sliced onions and garlic: stunted vegetables that in the States were left in the fields at harvest. Johnny would have brought a chain of garlic heads the size of tangerines, if he had known. Or grapes, since he noticed those in the markets were dried up. "Too expensive," his father said. "No one buys them. The rich can afford to get them from Hong Kong on their trips."

It wrenched Johnny's heart to watch his father doing the work of servants in that house; for he remembered that even water had been served to the doctor there, and his slippers were brought down to the clinic at the end of the day.

"Where is he?" Johnny referred to the young man in *sando*.

"Left the other day," the doctor said, clearing the counter. "No one wants to be houseboy any more. If they can find no other work, they will come for a week, then leave again to load trucks or clean fish in the market. He said he gets thirty pesos a day; but since he pays for room and board, it's not enough. However, for him it's exciting work. Here, he's confined. Servants have no sense of duty any more. Or loyalty. Some even rob you. This one is not a steady worker, but he is honest. So he would come, I gave him money for his bus fare here, and some extra to leave to his parents. That means nothing any more to them, though.''

Johnny's thoughts paced back and forth in his mind while his father talked.

"What do you do, Johnny?'' His father had to repeat the question.

He stammered out the answer. "Radiation, Papá. Therapy.'' His arms were bristling with sweat which ran down to his fingers. "I have not unpacked. I'd better.'' Johnny stood up, suddenly uncomfortable.

"Didn't you want to be a chemical engineer?''

Johnny could not recall, had no wish to have every sequence in his life played back to him right then. "I switched to physics at U.P. Don't you remember, Papá? And I went to the States to go on to high intensity physics.'' He pulled a deep breath. He might as well continue. "My adviser suggested radiation therapy—his field. I got a job right away at Worcester City. It's all about....''

"Bombarding cells with radiation to force them to behave.'' His father beat him to the explanation. "Do you have any regrets?''

Johnny stopped to think before shaking his head. "I'll go unpack, Papá.''

His father followed him to the bedroom, watched him open the suitcases, begin taking out his things. "I have regrets, but it's too late.''

Not you, Papá, he wanted to say, but could not. The gaps in their lives could not be crossed over with such platitudes. Everything between them had to matter in order to make up for the time lost to distance, to the absence from each other's thoughts.

"Something worth the trouble of living,'' his father was saying. "Like memory. I can't remember your mother that clearly, our life together. All I can see are the patients I had, their faces exchanging bodies; patients and grief. That can't be all...."

Something worth the trouble of living in connection with what? Johnny wondered.

"After the funeral for the boy Rio...."

Yes, he had regrets, Johnny concluded, opening himself to scrutiny. But they were, more properly, disappointments. Mostly when he had arrived in the States, after the flush of expectation. He had thought everything would be better there, everyone fair and aboveboard. No one trying to get away with anything, get something for nothing, grab, usurp. No underhandedness, manipulation. But there was all that and the prejudice. The newspapers—without hysteria— reported licensing boards being bribed, dishonest elections: that Chicago election of Kennedy, for instance. Yet the system worked, was not overrun by corruption, and there was freedom if you were willing to demand it. With some courage to be oneself, not another Anglo—one's own name and one's own face—one carved out this freedom that brought its own peace.

"It occurred to me", his father continued. "Here I am retired almost twenty-seven months, too long doing nothing...."

"I intended to come to Rio's funeral," Johnny explained, "but Martin...." He could not think of an excuse, let alone a reason. Why not just say, I don't want to hear about your failures and hurts, Papá?

"At the funeral, I realized I have become really old. I also decided that while I breathe, something must be expected of me. I can't tell what. I'm too old and full of regrets." His father stood there, looking at Johnny's clothes on the bed as if he were seeing another patient coiled in pain, moaning.

"No, you're not, Papá," Johnny said, his hands full of

socks he could not find a place for in the wardrobe.

"It's terrifying. Worse than an illness, a terminal disease, because no one recovers from being old." His father sat down on the bed, so light that the bed did not sag from his weight.

Johnny felt old, too; as if that were a beast deep inside him that leapt and recognized the other inside his father. He felt even older, as he wondered what the situation called for so he could act properly and nobly, though he felt himself to be far away.

"The other day, when I went to see you at the hotel, I wanted your opinion. I don't think either Martin or you want this house...."

There was no way to agree with that, Johnny sensed, without appearing to renounce his father. It was the truth but he could find no way to assent to it. "You do what you will, Papá. Don't worry about Martin or me."

"Then I'll go ahead with my plan." His father got up, walked to the door but turned around to say, "You know, *hijo*, I want to repay those who have been kind to me, but they are all dead. I remember the barber in our town who gave me a haircut knowing I had not even half a coin in my pocket. And an old woman—I call her old when, at that time, she was younger than I am now—who sold *puto* and when she saw me, wrapped a piece of the rice cake in a banana leaf. 'Just a taste,' she would say, though the piece was as big as the ones for sale. People who did not have much and still shared what they had. That's why I could not charge my patients. I did not even want to accept the vegetables they grew and gave to me, for they could have sold them for their needs. I did not have society patients, *hijo*. That disappointed your mother, I think. Then she got used to it. I can't remember what I started to say...."

"About repaying kindnesses, Papá."

"Yes, that's it. Since all those people are dead, I could

give back what they gave me by turning this house into a free clinic. Or let's say, by practising among the squatters. I'm not afraid...."

"Of what, Papá?

"You know, if you treat the poor, you're suspected of being subversive. But they can do what they want with me. That's the beauty of it. I'm not afraid to die. And even better, it will be no great loss if they kill me the way that doctor in Samar was killed for working in the *barrios*. Bobby de la Paz. He kept on despite the threats. Gunned down in his clinic. Clean getaway...."

"It sounds great, Papá, but perhaps there's another way...."

"We'll talk about it more, tomorrow. You're tired and it's late." His father closed the door carefully after himself.

The closing sounded like the bark of a dog from nowhere, because Johnny wanted to hear everything right away. The morning was too long to wait; he was ready to respond with affection and enthusiasm now.

A real dog's barking came from inside the yard. Johnny opened the door, walked down the hall to the front window. His father was going down the stairs to check.

It was Martin.

"I'll let him in, Papá," Johnny offered. "Wait inside." He had a vague sense of protecting his father, and was prepared to do so for the rest of his life.

"There's a special way of turning the lock...."

"I know, Papá." Johnny ran past his father on the steps. The dog Halcon was barking his tail off. Johnny held the dog by the collar until it recognized Martin. "Quiet, boy. That's enough."

"I decided to stay for the night. At least since you're here. Papá still up?" Martin locked his car before entering.

"He's waiting," Johnny lied.

There was something cheerful in the house now; an

energy, something becoming complete. It was confirmed by his father's welcome at the door, as if both of them had just come in together. It ceased to matter that one of them was born in the clinic to a young girl who had slipped out before morning. Was Martin ever told? Or did his brother pay attention to such things? Had it crossed their father's mind since, and did he remember which child was his?

Johnny did not linger on these thoughts. A rare feeling of everything being in place drew him into the house, after his father and brother. He sensed that from now on, it would not be empty again.

Tired out of his mind and aching all over, Johnny Manalo nevertheless listened to his brother, to the pauses that lengthened finally into sleep, leaving Johnny in that early Friday morning to figure out why Martin would insist on taking care of the Pete Alvarez incident—such a callous word for death—unless he figured on wresting Leticia, and perhaps Sylvia as well, from Walter's protection.

On the way to his old room down the stairs, having ceded Martin his bed, Johhny stopped for a glass of water. There on the dining table was an unfinished game of solitaire, the columns neatly lined up with each card covering only the lower edge of the one above. From being shuffled too many times, the set had become limp.

I could have brought Papá a pack of playing cards, Johnny reflected, ashamed of his thoughtlessness. The Harvard Coop had fancy plastic-coated sets imported from France. Not just a pack, but several to last the old man's lifetime. Why had he not?

Setting the glass of water on the table, Johnny studied the cards to see if his father, overtaken by sleep, had stopped in the middle of the game, or if the solitaire was dead. The possibility of finishing what his father had started excited

Johnny out of drowsiness as one card opened another until only the three cards in his hand remained to be played: the queen of diamonds, the king of clubs and beneath, the three of diamonds. No way to pull out the three since the king was under the queen. Just three cards left but the way they came up killed the game.

Johnny decided to play solitaire on his own before turning into his room. One game led to another as he tried to get not just one but three consecutive sets. Close to making it, he was tempted to cheat. While he played, the past was neatly disconnected from the moment. Day One was when he had arrived at Manila International Airport.

Sitting in the silence of the house and tamed by the monotony of turning up card after card when it had ceased to matter any more, Johnny did not recall going down to his own room. But there in the morning, his father knocked to wake him.

"Ready for breakfast?"

After he figured out where he was, Johnny hurried out of bed, showered and dressed quickly so he could share in the plans for the clinic.

Martin greeted him, "Papá and I discussed the clinic. I persuaded him to set one in the squatter area so he won't have to give up the house. Do you take sugar in your coffee?"

"What about the house?" Johnny asked, sitting between his brother and his father.

"Papá can rest here. So he won't always be on call." Martin answered for his father. "I never liked coming into the house and meeting strangers downstairs."

"Martin is right," his father said. "Your mother felt the same way. She did not come out of her room until all the patients had gone. It makes sense."

Johnny felt upset that nothing had been left for him to help decide. Though he might have come to the same conclusion, he wanted the chance to put in a word. As if he and his brother had been repelling negative charges, Johnny turned his back to Martin.

"No time to waste," Martin dragged his chair away from the table. "I'll start the car while you finish breakfast."

His father pushed his own chair under the table, leaned over to collect the spoons and stack the dishes. "Turn the lights off, *hijo*." His father's hurry was evident in the way he brushed off Halcon, who stood in his way, expecting the usual attention.

Johnny followed, feeling like someone tagging along. From the back seat of Martin's car, he watched the neighbors' houses give way to shops and stores just before entering the main road. Then across it, into *Heroes del 96*, with goats bleating all over the road toward Libis, running on legs as sharp and thin as twigs, furiously chewing their cuds, ears twitching with mischief as they darted just ahead of the car only to stop short, heads lifted for some scent, so infuriating Martin that he blasted his horn.

Some king of the road. Johnny mocked his brother in his thoughts, pleased with the idea of his brother running his freshly scrubbed tires over the beaded droppings of the goats.

The road became a path as it descended, sloping unevenly towards the fishponds beyond which lay the river with its fringe of trees. Ruts that had formed during the past year's rains, by trucks that had dumped the squatters on top of the garbage, appeared like the tracks of animals that had disappeared.

It was your suggestion to come here, Johnny chided his brother silently. He could see nothing to commend the place.

Wild sunflower and *lantana* came close to crossing the path in several places the way brambles hid Snow White's sleeping place. Or was it Sleeping Beauty's glass bed?

Ampalaya vines climbed fences of twigs and dried branches, staking a haphazard claim to the land. Over these, laundry hung from thorns. Unexpectedly a clearing would appear, a piece of open flat ground where children in various stages of undress shrieked at play or stalked red dragonflies.

Martin's sleek white car sparked the children's interest. Some attempted to run alongside. One lifted up an arm with a stone. As the doctor was recognized, the arm slowly came down, stone still held tightly.

Then houses, or what passed for houses. One or two older ones were set back under still older trees, different from the new huts built of wooden crates, which opened right out into the path. Between them the alleys were as narrow as the lines of stepping stones set into the mud that had dried, waiting for the rains.

They passed a *sari-sari* store with a few jars of sweets, a string of bananas, matches, cigarettes. As small as it was, it had a sign advertising soft drinks, incorporating the proprietor's name in block letters, white against the background of red.

The squatters were still beyond this place. They had settled themselves on the garbage dumps the way a typhoon smashes communities together. Appropriate to the huddle of makeshift huts there was an unfinished chapel and the tree. Slowly, Johnny recognized the place, remembered the occasion—Rio's wake.

"Park there," his father told Martin, rolling down the window. "That house there. What do you think? But it has the afternoon sun. It would be too hot for the patients, waiting."

"Let's look," Martin said, turning off the ignition. Through the heavy tint of the car window, it was hard to recognize the place. It looked like a crater that had recently exploded.

A woman with an infant on her hip walked by as they

were getting out of the car. Johnny felt mean, thinking her body might have come out of a fishing tackle box: it seemed to be all hooks. Was this his way of disengaging himself from the place?

Yet he might have found something more tender in that place if, like Martin, he had been sought for advice. This was the irrational aspect of himself that he wanted to be rid of, that made him bleed before he was ever wounded.

Johnny felt disinherited and disowned when, as they walked, his father placed a hand on Martin's shoulder. Perhaps it was only natural rebellion delayed into the dead zone of middle age.

Other goats took over the center of the clearing into which the chapel opened. Flies with dark heavy bodies zoomed across their path on green wings, feasting on the droppings that rolled in the dust.

As if wired to his father and brother, Johnny followed them to the threshold of the first hut. What had happened to Sylvia Mendez' homing device that allowed her to zero in on him wherever he was? Had she lost interest or was she in deeper trouble than he imagined?

It hurt all over that he had not seen her since Wednesday night at the birthday dinner. Close to forty hours felt like centuries to him. This free-running pain could make any place look like a sprawling emptiness. Pain seemed to be the message of his heart and his brain.

Watching intently with their bodies, children stood around them—those bodies looking curiously used, second-hand. Harvard Square clothing stores had found the word: "experienced".

Finally, a woman came out in response to their call. Her dress was one big wrinkle with torn pockets that sagged with the weight of her hands. Streaked with white, her hair looked to Johnny like electrode wires registering shocks and impulses. After asking them in, though there was not enough space for them to enter, she took both hands from her pockets and placed an arm behind her, grasping the other at the elbow.

It turned out that she could not speak for the owners, who were not at home. She thought, however, that the room they were interested in was being saved for a brother in Bataan. "When they found out it was a nuclear reactor being built in their town, he wanted to come here, for the children's sake." She pointed to the barbershop on the ground floor of the next hut. "The *barangay* captain might be able to help you."

Then following them as if unwilling to part with their company, she continued, "We are all poor here, Doctor. It will not be worth your time."

The *barangay* captain gave up his turn at the barber's single chair to talk to them. He was about Johnny's age. Though his shirt was thin and he wore slippers, he looked satisfied with himself—pleased in fact. His manner indicated he knew, was anxious to have it known by everyone, that everything that happened in that sunburned place had to pass through his hands, at his leisure.

He offered them land on which to build without stating what right he had to it. "I'll show it to you. The rent will be reasonable. Protection goes with it. I'll even sleep in the clinic if necessary."

Stopping to light a local cigarette, he gave them the courtesy of offering them the pack first. Martin refused by looking down at the pack of Benson & Hedges 100s in his pocket.

"America's favorite," the *barangay* captain said, to prove he had read the ads. "They must taste terrific."

Without returning the courtesy of offering his own pack, Martin went straight to the point. "We are not planning to build. It might not work. My father is not young any more."

"Why not?" Johnny came up on the other side of the

barangay captain, ready to throw everything on building because Martin did not want to. "It is the better idea. There is nothing here that a storm will not topple over at the first blow."

Encouraged, the *barangay* captain brought up the difficulties of renting. "In town a room smaller than the one you looked at would rent for eight hundred. Here, we can waive some of the regulations, since I trust you."

Martin stepped back to his father. The knowing look they exchanged posed the question even Johnny guessed: Did the man expect his palm to be greased? "I see," the doctor said, divulging no more than what the two words said.

"The Ministry of Human Settlements might have its own clinic planned," the *barangay* captain said, walking ahead. "But I'll do everything I can for you. I'll take care of the permits, all the red tape. In fact, I will even provide you with the laborers. Masons. Carpenters. Some men are out of work...."

The lot they stopped at was overrun with sunflowers and *talahib* at the edge of the dump, mostly on a slope.

"Rent as much or as little as you want."

"I had a more central location in mind," the doctor said.

Johnny could see that it would not work. There was no electricity in all that place, no running water or telephone.

"I'll make it easy for you to build," the *barangay* captain said. "How much do you want to give a month? We can come to an agreement. I'm not a difficult man and I can see that you aren't either."

"We'll think about it," Martin said. "We'll let you know."

"I hoped we could come to an agreement now. We need work in this place. The priest, he's not really a priest since he ordained himself, his family gave him the money for the chapel, but he can't find cement, so men are out of work. Just waiting."

That had nothing to do with him, Johnny thought, looking

in all directions except toward the official. The sky looked bruised above the dikes of fishponds.

"He wears a soutane like a regular priest. He baptizes, if anyone is willing to have him baptize their children. He has not performed a wedding yet. No one is crazy enough to ask him...."

"Whether he's ordained or not, he appears to be a saintly person," the doctor said, cutting in. "What he is or is not, is between God and himself. I'm sure God has forgiven worse sins, if that is a sin."

"I have nothing against him, Doctor," the *barangay* captain toned down his words. "The statues in his church are supposed to be miraculous. The poor believe....well, you know how the poor are. We are all poor here but some are poorer than others." The *barangay* captain sat hunched over the trail, forcing them to reconsider.

Johnny walked some distance toward the fishponds.

"The miraculous statue is that of the Immaculate Conception. Find out for yourself if her eyes really follow you. Not just one person, but several at the same time. A real miracle. What do you say about this lot? I might get another offer...."

"Then again, you might not," Martin said. "Let's go, Papá. Johnny."

The *barangay* captain laughed. "Yes, sir. You're right. But I might be right, too."

"We'll let you know," Martin said decisively. "Come on, Papa. Let's have lunch and decide later."

"This afternoon, I will be at Malacañang. That's why I was getting a haircut, so I won't look poor," the *barangay* captain said. "We're being called. The Batasan elections in May. We'll get instructions, and brown envelopes to make sure we follow those instructions to the letter." He stood up to follow them, still trying to ingratiate himself. "Boy," he said, "that sun is as hot as a woman's tongue. I never fight women, we can't win against them." He laughed at his own joke.

"If not taking the lot means I won't have a clinic here," the doctor mused. "I should pass by Rio's family...."

"Let's wait, Papá. Actually, squatters are not the safest neighbors. Any number and kind of fugitives hide among them. The New People's Army recruits here. Men from the NPA's sparrow or execution unit once escaped in tricycle cabs right through the cordon of army and police—Keystone Cops! Right in Manila, Johnny."

As Martin opened the car door for their father, the angle of the sun fired his hair. Johnny noticed how red it was, pale clay. Martin had to be the one born in the clinic, a foreigner's leavings. This last thought, unprovoked, took all the pleasure out of Johnny's discovery.

Johnny took the time to walk toward the open door of the chapel but did not enter. Inside, a woman was rubbing her back against the man-high crucifix, turning slowly about, the way the earth circles the sun, sealing her pores with what she believed were the statue's powers.

"Come on, Johnny," Martin called out, impatient to be off.

Johnny got into the back seat. Trying to have his brother disowned was not the same as having himself claimed. The full record of himself was in the brain—or mind (which?)—the whole truth of himself from birth; from before his birth, when he spurted out to swim into his own fluids. How did he get that truth out? Was it even a single truth or had it been parcelled out to different parts of his body in order to frustrate retrieval by an enemy; the body shrewdly, willfully refusing to give up its secret, even of recent memory.

To celebrate what had been left undecided, Martin treated them to lunch at Alfredo's. His father had not eaten there.

"Steak is too rich for my stomach," his father said, choosing fish: "It feeds the brain."

Johnny listened while his father explained why fish was fine for thinking. For him, steak was not special—he could broil one any time in Cambridge—but he went along with Martin's choice of tenderloin, reminded of Sylvia Mendez opening her mouth to receive the first bite of his dinner at the Silahis Hotel. That was only a week ago; but it seemed so far back, he actually had to dredge it from memory.

Only three weeks remained and he could predict that his father's clinic would be taking up all that time.

The disturbing and somewhat irrelevant memory of Sylvia Mendez turned his inevitable departure into certain disaster. He did not look forward to leaving.

"We'll have to rethink the clinic, Papá," Martin said. "It's become more complicated than it has to be."

Johnny could not enter into the discussion. Though he relished the sizzling steak on the wooden platter, he also knew that no distraction or drug could touch the pain he felt because Sylvia Mendez had gone out of his life. The thought went through his body like a catgut being pulled through his flesh.

"Is it good?" Martin wanted compliments. Johnny nodded. "The fish is very good," his father said, cutting off a piece so Johnny could try it.

Johnny accepted, thinking that there was no reason at all for him to invest with such strong feelings things not within his control. Whether or not Sylvia Mendez re-entered his life, whether or not his father rented or built his clinic should not make much difference to him. He was not like Rose Quarter, too sensitive for the world, every cell fighting for survival at the least scrape of her skin.

Unaided, Johnny's thoughts returned to Rose Quarter. Was she watering the fig tree and the pot of wandering jew in the kitchen which was just an el, the table joining it to the dining area which was one end of the living room? Under the slant of the roof against which he regularly banged his head, the bathroom separated the tiny bedroom from the entry where he had bookcases lining the wall.

Some apartment, Martin would say. A squatter's hut in comparison with Walter's mansion.

And some friends! If Martin ever met them. One constantly complained so that Johnny, out of pique or pity, would drive him about; his eyes were supposedly too poor to drive at night and during the day his arthritis acted up—selectively. Once favors were extended, they had to be increased or this friend would feel betrayed. Each favor was the point of reference for the next. Johnny was envied even the occasional crimp in his back because it allowed him time off. Another friend thought only of converting old apartments and houses into condominiums which he would offer to Johnny as a favor at prices he couldn't afford. The third was not so bad. He only drank every bottle in Johnny's apartment, passing out and puking so that the little attic space was filled with a stench that would drive Johnny into Rose Quarter's place. Then there was Rick Fielder....

A man should be able to be honorable all by himself. Outside of his friends.

Johnny envied Father Armand. Imagine ordaining himself in defiance of the institutional church in order to perform its work. There was more than a little irrationality there. And perhaps a lot of innocence. And of all things, probably, faith. How could anyone tell? Or deny?

It was so easy to sum up lifetimes and relationships for the moment's advantage. With regard to himself, someone must have been kind and tender to him. Something good must have happened to him in the States besides those trips to the mountains—he climbed Mt. Washington on foot and by car—the ache that started between his eyes on seeing suddenly a lake buried between hills; something beautiful with no dependence upon his life. Tall ships coming in full majesty into Boston Harbor, sails blowing in the wind; the coastlines of Maine where the sea carried its waves straight into the center of coastal towns. And yes, someone's foresight and charity in donating portions of the shore for those who could not afford to live in mansions with private beaches.

While he entertained these thoughts, Johnny felt free of distrust and fear. Life stopped working its early ravages in complicity with death. That day everything seemed surmountable.

"Would you like to be brought home now, Papá?" Martin was asking.

Lost in his thoughts, Johnny did not catch the point of reference and, guilty for withdrawing into himself so that he could not remember that moment with his brother and father, he decided to pay them special attention, to respond instantly and fully to them. When the waiter came by with the check, he took it; but while he was taking out his wallet, Martin gave the waiter his gold credit card.

"The American wants to pay, Papá," Martin said. "Save your dollars, Johnny. We'll need it if we're forced to run to the States. Who knows! You'll be our Social Security, Johnny, so start investing in blue chips as soon as you return."

His father looked from him to Martin as if just discovering he had two sons.

Waiting for their escorts, a couple of young women walked in on extremely high heels, with hair down to their waists. They stopped where the clientele could appreciate them. A taxi driver came in and sat across from his fare, an American and his lady friend.

"Let's go," Martin said, with Johnny's coffee only half drunk.

A light feeling formed at once in Johnny's abdomen as

if a fight were about to break out. He remained at his seat: *he* was the son. He could see his thoughts racing as on a graph that recorded peaks and depressions.

Then, ashamed of his resentment, he hurried after his brother. Had he faked all of his feelings? Perhaps even the matter of the child being born in the clinic: had he willed Salud to narrate what was in his imagination? He was life-set in his own pool of inertia, with obsessions as rigid and insignificant as any Martin had.

Hardly anyone spoke on the way to his father's house. At the gate, his father watched them turn around and leave after letting him out. To Johnny, the frail figure looked like someone buried in a common grave.

It seemed far-fetched to Johnny, the lengths to which Martin was insisting on going to take care of Sylvia Mendez, and how he was still talking about Leticia after admitting it was over between them.

Rambling like a man who has just walked out of an empty house, who would not live past his next birthday, Martin re-crossed his paths, taking back everything he had said about the sisters.

Clarity and confusion fought for Johnny's attention, driving him back into his own thoughts. He wanted to be free of them so he could listen to his brother, but without his thoughts he could feel his juices traveling the distance between his organs, forcing their way with primitive strength impossible to bear.

Johnny did not want to have to contend with that at the moment. Nor with guilt about Pete having been killed, so Martin said, to test Johnny's reaction—to see how far he would go to protect Sylvia, what resources he had going for him.

He got irritated at Martin for saying that. In all likelihood,

Pete Alvarez was killed for making a nuisance of himself, for crashing the party and for encouraging Sylvia to run on the opposition ticket.

Trying to get those things off his mind, Johnny concentrated on the scene outside. He was most safe when he felt no sensations. Right then he felt his body to be racing, all pulses whipping about until their wavelengths phased together.

"Let's settle the clinic," he urged Martin, to keep him from digressing onto Sylvia Mendez. Corrosive to his desire to be congenial for the rest of his visit was the impulse—obsession, really—to get everything decided and settled. The desire to have nothing bothering his mind kept him jumping, in the States, from one problem to another, aiming to be free thereafter; but new problems came up and it was impossible to get ahead of his life. Johnny Manalo, choosing modest ambitions immodestly, allowed his imagination to take over, boxed himself in with unnecessary anxieties.

"Papá will get sick in the squatter area," Martin said, as if it had not been his idea in the first place. "Take him to Boston, instead. Travel with him. If you agree to be courier for some people I know, you can travel everywhere, any time. You don't have any commitments to tie you down. But here, in a clinic in that God-forsaken place, Papá will only get caught in some dragnet."

"And you do have commitments. You certainly have!" Johnny was scornful. He felt transparent, someone whose thoughts had been filmed and were being played back on a wide screen. Occasionally he thought that what he was seeing was being played back this way inside his skin. Another of his madnesses. Like refusing to get married. But he was married, in a manner of speaking. There was the ring he had bought Rose Quarter from Shreve, Crump and Low when the same carat would have cost half as much at the jewellers inside the brick buildings on Washington Street on the way to Government Center. But that was in place of the three thousand she could have charged him—going rate as of two years before. It was not a wedding ring but a friendship ring.

Caught in the frenzy of his own thoughts, Johnny missed hearing Martin's caustic reply that was followed instantly by remorse. "Let's compromise, Johnny."

Sensing his advantage, Johnny almost said, "I don't make deals." But didn't he?

"Before you say anything, listen. I love Papá as much as you do. I want a clinic for him if that is what he wants and what is good for him. And if he wants to get married...."

Johnny tuned him out. He could not think of his father getting married again.

"Okay?" Martin went on to talk about their being the only two in the world, who should help each other.

"Okay," Johnny agreed, just to cut short the discussion, to shut his brother up. All that "Walter wants to meet you" stuff was just another hype, a come-on. He was not going to play their games, not even for Sylvia Mendez. Let them say he was at odds even with himself. It was true he rarely had a clear perception of where he was. Out of fear that he would not be able to take himself as he was, he allowed things to resolve themselves. Unable to dissolve the marriage on his own initiative, unwilling to face a confrontation or to accept Rose Quarter forever, he coasted along. Resting easy in toleration left him adrift. But what could he do? That was the way he was.

He saw a man picking up scraps from a garbage can. "There should be soup kitchens," he said, glad enough to change the subject.

"Madame won't hear of it. She maintains that there are no poor or hungry. It's paradise here, didn't you know?"

Johnny did not reply. The metal footholds on the lamp posts were bracketing the scenes as they sped along, providing him with a distraction that inhibited shock.

It was not where he would have chosen that Sylvia Mendez find him, but when Johnny got back to his father's house, there she was talking to his father in the garden.

He did not take the time to bring Martin's car inside the gate but parked it alongside the fence where the yellow *campanilla* grew into the bougainvilleas, tricking the eye with disparate leaves and buds.

"Hi," she greeted him, walking to the gate ahead of his father. "Your father has been entertaining me with stories about you and Martin."

"She won't come into the house, *hijo*", his father explained. "Says she prefers gardens to sitting rooms. It turns out, *hijo*, that I once went to their house in Santa Mesa. I knew her father, but this was a long time ago. I did not know he had died."

"Your father came to treat Papá. He was never very well, as you know. And yet he was never so sick that he had to stay in bed. I don't know what it was. He never went to doctors. Said nothing in the world could keep a man alive any longer than his allotted time. Mamá must have sent for you or perhaps you merely came for a visit, Doctor."

They were talking to each other, and Johnny felt he had come unexpected once more into his father's house.

"Come in," his father said, speaking to both of them.

"Another day, Doctor. Today, I'm in a hurry. I just have something to tell Johnny, then I'll go." She stepped closer to his father and kissed him on the cheek, her hands clinging to his shoulders for the support that was not there.

"I'll expect you then, when you can come," his father said, leaving the door open after going in. "Come any time, *hija*."

"Well," Sylvia Mendez turned around as if she might kiss Johnny on the cheek, too. "I asked Martin's secretary and she gave me the address. I was afraid Martin would also be here....Aren't you going to say something, Johnny? Anything happen since the last time?''

"I guess not," was all he could say, looking at her as if she were an apparition.

"Walter has left. Leticia and I are flying to San Francisco this evening. I think we're meeting Walter some place, then just keep going until after the elections, at least. But you know how plans are.''

The words Johnny wanted to say were a mass of earth-worms tunnelling inside his brain. He could neither fake a response nor improvise an excuse for being dumbfounded by her being there and by what she was saying. It was certainly not what he had feared would happen. He was sweating inside his shirt and all he could think of was that he should shower before talking to her.

"If you have nothing to say, Johnny Manalo, I'll go. It was nice knowing you. Maybe we'll run into each other sometime." Her face was just a breath away as she spoke taunting him with her smile, like a burst from some wayward galaxy.

It was not the conversation he wanted, all on her side and about to end while he could only look past her to see if another lily had opened, if its yellow center was darker this time or awash with light. There were only leaves cupping the shadows of leaves above. Though he stood there waiting for what else could happen, he might as well have run from her, for he was afraid and also angry that she did not respond to what he felt, only to how he acted and what he failed to say.

He looked up and what he saw appeared to him to be pieces of flesh impaled on the branches by birds, entrails and eyes where insects might have laid their eggs, for these seemed to be stirring with the furtiveness of new life, swarming.

Powerful rhythms and blunt melodies surged through him, forcing him to shiver where he stood while she walked past him, not out of the garden but deeper into it. He could have said, "I'm glad you came," but that would sound insincere in its ordinariness. The slow movement of his emotions into thought, however, permitted nothing better. No words came as she walked ahead, burning the path with her footsteps.

"Yes," he called after her, assenting to what he thought he heard. What he really wanted to know was if she had shot Pete Alvarez. The plants in the garden looked like strange out-croppings, could answer no questions.

"Yes?" She did not stop but moved where the plants appeared to have been rearranged, leaves and flowers like panels of fabric hung to cover up holes.

So unreal were the feelings Sylvia Mendez was pulling out of him that he might have been the guest in the garden, unsure of where to head. Each step he took amounted to a first entry, full of hesitations. Woodwinds and strings might have been playing under the trees, their music rising and falling with his thoughts. The real garden was elsewhere.

Violent scenes began roughing his mind: yachts loaded with gold bullion colliding in the ocean; Filipinos with gold bound for Swiss banks, losing their way on the high seas....

What could he say to her, what answers did she expect? She who loved gardens and lonely old priests. "Did I tell you about my father confessor? He was seventy, could barely see, but I loved him. I went to confession week after week just to hear him say the words of absolution. I made up sins...." Gardens and old priests and complicated lives lived simply. He was light-years away from it all. And what about Pete Alvarez? It would be like fighting air turbulence, living with her or inside her skin.

"Did I tell you about the wax altar my mother had?" She

had stopped, encouraging him on. Ferns spilled their spores into the sunlight. "A wax altar from New Orleans. A French concoction. Fine lace on the bodices of angels and saints. It might have been secretly brought out during the French Revolution. You know, when nuns were beheaded at the guillotine. Have you read the book of memoirs—fictional of course—*Song of the Scaffold*? A young nun who had escaped, watching the others trying to sing right up to the executioner. Then silence: the words dying in their throats. The young nun, watching, took up the song and gave away who she was. I read that some church statues—churches were gutted in the fervor too—were buried like corpses to save them from burning. But this wax altar had always to be kept in cool rooms or it would melt. It's terribly hot, isn't it?"

"It is," Johnny found two words to reply to her. To admit heat and sleeplessness would not kill him. Besides, he wanted to hear more about the altar while he stood where crickets called from underneath leaves, tossing their song into the lily pond with such assurance. He felt like tumbling on the grass, prolonging expectations. "It's been very hot," he said. He did not want it to end. Was there not a way she could live in that garden, forever stand there where she stood?

"Well, I must go." Sylvia Mendez looked up at the sky as if she had felt a raindrop, her neck gently repeating the soft movement of the wind among the leaves. "Walter would not be pleased to know I'm here. I was the one he wanted to marry. He asked Papá but I was only sixteen and Letts was of age. Walter knows you and Letts mated under the *seresa* tree. That's his word, exactly what he said. I can't stand the way he looks at me...."

She had thrown another ten things at him and he was left trying to untangle them, put them in sequence so he could respond properly. Was it she or Walter who had been betrayed—or himself? He could have held her there, but it was his father's garden and his father's house. What was he to say or do?

"I envy you, Johnny," she said passing him on the walk, her heels finding every crack between the stones. "You can be anything you want, do whatever you want....Is that not a *cabique*? I thought there was none left in the world...."

Somehow, as if he had weathered a climate of long days, he managed to say, "My father planted it, this is the only property he owns." The logic of what he said felt close to the heart of all their lives—until he spoke the words.

"Well, I like your father and his garden...." She was speaking, who lived like a plant in the sun, nothing else demanded of her but to be. The atoms in her body, their bodies, had come from those first unleashed when the world exploded into existence. But it was not true that he could have anything he wanted, because he wanted her to remain in that garden forever, and he knew it could not be so.

"Johnny, this is crazy. Absolutely crazy. Will you marry me?" She laughed even as she asked, the laughter of someone afraid, making a show of herself, walking exaggeratedly to the swing of some primal tide to feel herself alive and there.

There was that silence, the silence in which he and his father before him had stood.

Then she ran toward the gate past the garden, ran to her car while everything disappeared for Johnny. He felt as helpless as someone trying with the eye alone to discover the composition of a raindrop or of fire. How could someone who saw only molecules where a rainbow descended or felt the palpitations of the heart instead of its subtle motions ever find the right word to say?

He ached, recalling the time he had walked up a hill with another girl who pulled his hand off her waist but did not run when accidentally he held it against her breast. Each of them might have been waiting for the same thing, reaching the top without having guessed what was on the other's mind. He knew this now, this possibility that softened the intransigence of stars for him. But not then, and not again, perhaps.

"Has she left?" his father asked from inside the house as Johnny stood outside the door.

"Yes," Johnny replied, coming in. He was torn at the core, a star so dense it pulled light to its own darkness.

"She's very nice," his father said, opening the door wide, as if someone else were coming in after Johnny. "Some day, perhaps, you'll settle down here and find a nice girl, *hijo*."

It was not the thought to hearten him while he felt the ache of not having given her an answer, an explanation. What, finally, did she think of him?

For a while yet he stood at the window, looking out but seeing her garden where she walked, stopping to recall her sister...all of her dead who had once been beautiful and free of the earth's rotation; whose lives were like bursts of fire flaring out. Then he turned away from that garden where she could not exact a promise from one who loved her with the elemental pull of suns.

He felt like someone who had been born without hands. But was it possible to reach out to Sylvia who was somewhere lost among the words she was saying?

They had toast and butter. And hot chocolate, which his father made from dark round cakes of cocoa the way Salud used to do. He churned it with the wooden stick Salud used, making it froth. It was too rich for Johnny, accustomed as he had become to instant cocoa stirred into hot water in the winter and cold milk in the summer. But he accepted a second cup. As he drank, he began to feel that something had been fulfilled because, at least, Sylvia Mendez had come.

154

Because she had come, she would again.

"This is the way your mother drank chocolate. Bear Brand cream and *churros*. I liked it with *carabao* milk. Lots of sugar, even *panocha* will do. Poured into rice with *paksiw* for breakfast. She thought I was a barbarian. She was high class, don't you see? I was the *puto maya* class. I preferred *puto maya* to *churros*. In the province, when I was a little boy, they cooked *malagkit* all day on the open fire. Their arms stiffened from stirring the sticky sweet rice, but that slow stirring made it special."

"I like both," Johnny answered although he had no clear memory of either. Toast and butter was more his style. Or pancakes from a mix. Lately he had been going to Mac-Donald's for breakfast on the way to his classes. Eggs on an English muffin with hash brown potatoes, for which he was inconsolably homesick already. It was not only the fast food served in plastic boxes, but the anonymity, the absence of expectations that lured him.

"I thought she would come in for a cup," his father said. "I'm sure she would have liked it. She reminds me of your mother, not in the face, but in something I can't tell. These are your mother's favorite cups. Do you remember?"

Johnny turned the cup around. He did not. Everything was new but also old in that house.

"She had the *Kastila* traditions. Her family dropped their final *d* and wanted her to go to Madrid and marry there. Eiroas. Just enough color in their skin and broadness in their nostrils to make them unhappy. A slight pull at their eyes, which I thought was interesting. It's how features are recombined in offspring, infinitely blended, that fascinates me. Each one is a unique combination. If no fingerprints match, should people? But some, who put much pride in how they look, want to be perfectly reproduced in their children. But even more fascinating than the infinite possibilities is how God keeps track of each one of us...."

"What else did Mamá like?" Johnny asked, wishing that moment to last, wondering whom he resembled of his mother's family, of his father's. From the way his father was talking, he was almost certain it was Martin who had been born in the clinic; but then it was he, not Martin, whose birth had crippled their mother.

"Bells in the trees and fine small cages of birds. Don't you remember? Cages all over the garden. After a few days, she'd let them go. Then I got her new ones."

Johnny lifted up his cup for his father to refill. "She could have married someone who would build her a mansion in Forbes. I don't know why she chose me or why she was happy in this house." His father laid the wooden churn on a plate rimmed with blue.

"Why couldn't she walk? I don't remember seeing her walk, Papá." Johnny asked even if the price of knowing would be guilt.

"She had an operation to remove a growth in her spinal nerve. The surgeon had such a reputation, too, so the accidental slicing...how can it be explained? Human error or the will of God, though I can't believe God wills such things."

They both glanced toward her room. When she was alive, her door was always open so she could see what was going on, hear them all going and coming. Her friends came sometimes. They had *merienda* in the room. Schoolmates from years back. They would recall the nuns who taught them literature, algebra, biology, every subject in terms of sin and hell and the fear of God, which alone could save their souls. He and Martin sat on her bed and listened or played marbles on the floor while the women talked, while some visiting child watched or played with its dolls or toy cars. One time, a little girl cut paper dolls under the table with its white cloth. Intrigued, he and Martin had tried to peek, but every time they lifted an edge of the tablecloth, she had screamed.

"I saved her jewels, *hijo*. I might as well give you your share. Martin took his already. Pour yourself another cup—I wonder if it's still warm—while I get the box."

Johnny got up to follow his father into his room but opened the door to his mother's room instead. It looked even more bare than the first time. On the floor below her bed was a shadow. To Johnny it could have been a cat that had simply lain down and died. He did not enter.

"Here." His father was out in the hall again, carrying an open box. "I thought...I've been thinking...that if you wanted, you could settle here and have the house. Your mother liked the garden. Most of the plants are hers, from her mother's garden. She could make anything grow, from tiny slips."

Johnny looked into the box without taking it. He had no eye to appreciate stones except by their size. He recalled that she wore jewels even in bed, slept with them....

"They looked good on her," his father said, looking down into the box. "She made them look even more precious. Jewels and the garden made her happy. *Vanidosa*, I teased her. She did her hair up with combs inset with pearls and other stones. Then she had matching earrings, pendants, bracelets, rings, brooches. I could give her nothing else but stones and plants. Nothing else. She could not have children...."

What he heard tore like crystal passing through Johnny's veins. "I thought Martin was the one born in the clinic, Papá...."

His father sat down, the open box still in his hands, realising the hurt of those words only after Johnny spoke. "We did not love you less, *hijo*. I thought you knew...."

"That's all right, Papá." He was struggling to forget what he had heard, willing to begin again with an empty heart. There was no other way: he was his own future and past.

"From the day you were born, you were with us...."

"Both of us, Papá?"

"Yes, *hijo*. Both times we accepted it as a miracle, directly from the hand of God."

"Yes, Papá. I understand."

"She held you in her arms and tried to suckle you. Some old wives' tale convinced her that she could, and she believed she did." His father covered his eyes with his hands.

Johnny had never been whipped by that hand or hers; but it might have been better if he had not been told, or had been told early enough, before he was capable of being hurt. And yet, sitting there, watching his father press the tears back into his eyes, Johnny felt love and wished he had not left, wished he had been in that house when she was dying. "Did she ask for me?"

"She waited for you. At the end she became blind, you know. Several small strokes, each taking a part of her. I thought I wrote. It was just as well. She was blind, so I could pretend to read letters from you. I bought her biscuits, the ones in the blue and white tin that she liked, and chocolates and other things. I told her they came from you. Silk scarves to cover her hair. At one point she lost all of it but it grew back, thick and curly. Very dark. I made her feel it. And she would ask, when she woke up, 'Bring me the scarf Juaniyo sent. The blue one.' It was as if she could tell their colors. I knew you would have sent them to her, if you had known that they would please her."

"Was she happy, Papá?"

"I tried to make her happy. She told me she was. I never cheated on her, *hijo*. Not while we were married and not after she died. Enough women tempted me, for their own reasons. But the point of any sacrifice—if that was what it was—is not that it is easy but because you love. And I was also happy. I think we are happy when we love someone.

158

For some, it is God."

Johnny drank the chocolate that had become cold and thick. "Did she think I came home?"

"Was coming. I would tell her to be patient and brave, because you were arriving in the morning, or that night. I said, 'Don't let go, Nena. Juaniyo is coming. He wants to see you.' It was selfish of me. She was suffering. She asked me to hold her. 'Tight,' she would say. Perhaps she wanted me to crush the breath out of her, for it to be over. We were praying the rosary, or rather, she was praying and I was responding with the beads in her hands. Partway through, the beads fell from her hands, her head dropped onto my shoulder....It was over. I held her as long as I could, trying to keep her warm—but it was no use."

"And Martin?"

"He was in Australia with some woman.... I'll let your brother tell you about his life, if he has not told you. I'm not very happy with some things. He wants to be rich. You know. When a person wants one thing that badly, then he will do anything. He's a partner in a pharmaceutical firm that imports, at a big discount I'm sure, drugs banned in the States. Drugs that eat you up inside, bringing you relief which you could have had if you waited for your body to fight back. And there's more.... But here, take the box, *hijo*."

"Thank you, Papá." Johnny closed it without looking into it.

"I was lucky, *hijo*. I went through a lot of hopelessness in my life, a lot of failures, but your Mamá and I felt each other's pain and hurt. We lived each other's life and so I can go on until my time comes. You and Martin gave us the happiness that comes from children. That made up for the many times in my life when I felt like a dying man. Until you experience that, you cannot appreciate life or understand why, if God did not exist, there is no reason to live.

Too many ideas, *hijo*. I don't know how they get into my head, but this is the reason I had better start the clinic. By the way, Father Armand was here."

"Father Armand?"

"He heard we were there and he came to offer his chapel until I can build the clinic. I like the man. I know he's not ordained by a bishop, but perhaps God knows this and if He allows it.... We do not have His wisdom."

"What did you say to him, Papá?" Johnny felt very tired and numb, as if wave upon wave had passed over him. Farthest from his mind was how many days to the hour he had been home, what time it was in Boston. Time had become single and one for him.

"I thanked him of course, with no intention then of accepting his offer. But while you and she were in the garden, it occurred to me that I could give you this house and build somewhere. Close to the clinic probably. Now, don't say anything yet. It's an old house, I know. There is Martin to ask first, by way of letting him know. What do you think?"

"I think we should return to the place and see it again before we decide."

"If you really want to go," his father said, but halfway down the stairs, stopped.

"What is it, Papá?"

"We have to give Father Armand time to think his offer over, *hijo*. Just in case he made it too hastily. We'll let him sleep over it and the first thing tomorrow morning...."

Johnny had no strong feelings either way. He wondered, however, if it was his father who needed time to decide, if this had anything to do with what the *barangay* captain had said about the priest being pressed by the squatters to divine a well out of garbage heaps—to draw healing waters out of the earth where the huts appeared like rat traps.

He looked up at the sky where the stars had not begun

160

to appear, where, unaided, the eye could not see the active galaxies exploding. Just as one cannot see, looking at a human being, the millions of molecules in each cell, splitting and straightening.

Trying to sleep that night, early to bed in preparation for the next morning's schedule, Johnny's thoughts wandered back to the stress management course on self-confidence as the key to success. But try as he might, Johnny was unable to think of anything good or positive about himself.

Nothing came to his mind. Wayward as always, his thoughts moved on to the blind musicians in the Kamayan restaurant at Padre Faura. With no shift in their attention, the patrons continued eating with their hands—a gimmick that drew those who wished to appear ultra-sophisticated. Johnny had watched them during one lunch, sportingly trying the customs of a life they disdained, fumbling with the rice, fingers deliberately inept.

The musicians in crisp white *barongs*, playing as if in seclusion, sang songs of separation and love unrequited, cradling their guitars and their violins, fingers like barbs on wire, framed by a deadly border of downcast eyes. Johnny Manalo saw himself in their midst: one full of memories, of repeated failings, of hungers that brought him nowhere.

These thoughts passed out of his mind soon enough—he had learned to program himself not to lose heart—but not before the blind musicians had reappeared to him as a row of sculpted corpses.

Waking up Saturday morning from nightmares he could not recall, Johnny Manalo thought of his return home as one continuously broken dream. He could hear his father moving around, so he decided to pack his bags. One suitcase had not even been unpacked, the other was almost ready.

In the pocket of a shirt he found the flyers given to him by the pump attendant at the Monument, the morning of the march from Malolos to protest the assassination of Benigno Aquino. They looked to him like some unintelligible genetic code, overlapping and degenerate signals for termination; he tossed them aside. As they fell, however, he saw Pete Alvarez' name beneath a poem, picked it up and saw another piece by him, describing another march when they were joined by the people from the towns they passed: "...We fed each other courage to face the military. Priests came out of their convents despite threats to keep away from the rallies, and they opened up churchyards for our assembly. We are becoming a flood," Pete wrote, "we will soon reach the gates. Whether these will be to heaven or to hell, we will soon discover."

Johnny turned the flyer to more poems at the back. Boxed in red was an item: "*Lakbayan Monitor*—Huge crowds greet and join Freedom Marchers in Meycauayan. About 15,000 are welcomed by crowds offering food and water, chanting boycott slogans. Concerned citizens join in the hundreds. Sr. Mariani of the Task Force Detainees speaks to the rally."

Another lost chance, Johnny thought. Here he was, planning to call Northwest Airlines and book his passage back, and he had missed the pulse of life in the country. He could have attended the Fact-Finding Board's investigation of the Aquino killing, or registered to boycott the elections as his father wanted to do....

He laid the flyers carefully on the table beside coins and keys, credit cards—props of a life that faced only its own daily struggle.

Yet he could not allow himself to become one of those who, at cocktail parties and fancy restaurants, ranted against government abuses. They only mocked the poor, whose misery they did not share, since they returned afterward to their estates and ivory towers, satisfied they had been heroic. Card-room patriots, hangers-on basking in the glow of what real protest brought about: demonstrators for the fun of it, in a modern *moro-moro*.

It was not in him, Johnny regretfully thought. He had failed to connect with Pete Alvarez while he had the chance, while his own self could have given way to the common self. Perhaps it was never possible. He saw the situation as a circular boundary he could not cross, used as he had become to life lived in boredom, relieved by minutiae that sometimes gave it a sense of being fulfilled. Perhaps he could still come out of that life, but it would involve a wrenching he did not know how to initiate. He would rather pack up and leave, try another time or have it forced upon him....

But he took the porous brown papers the flyers were printed on—even warehouse ads in the States were on thick glossy paper more proper to momentous announcements— and easing the folds carefully, placed them at the bottom of his suitcase. Someone in the States might find them interesting souvenirs. Someone whose mind was not too far away to connect with the surge for freedom.

At least Pete had done something with his life, made some kind of difference. Johnny did not expect to accomplish anything of the sort, being too set in his path to substitute dying for living. Nor did he even expect ever to puzzle out his life.

Turning down his collar, afraid of what conclusions he might reach, Johnny walked out into the hall.

His father had made breakfast. Toast and chocolate again. On the platter with blue edges there was ham and eggs, fried hard the way he always wanted them. Unpressed cloth napkins were thrust under the plates.

"What would you say if I said I had decided to accept Father Armand's offer?"

It took Johnny some time to recollect what the offer was. "That's great, Papá," he answered with the exuberance acquaintances exchange along with formal pleasantries.

"Let's go, then. I thought Martin would be coming along, too, but we can't wait all morning, *hijo*." His father got up from the table, placing all the contents of his plate into Halcon's dish in the kitchen. "As soon as Halcon finishes, we'll go." It did not take the dog long to polish off the hot rice into which the eggs had been stirred. "Let him out, *hijo*, while I get my hat."

Johnny decided not to tell his father yet about returning to the States. Waiting to be asked to back the car out of the garage, Johnny thought of Martin along with the young boy who had dangled blue rubber slippers on his toes, with the bird struggling inside the web, and his father telling him, "We did not love you less, *hijo*."

Once in the car, like someone determined not to let his mind wander through his prayers, Johnny fixed his attention on every word his father said.

It was already hot though only seven o'clock. Johnny looked up and about, as if he might see traces of his breath the way cold winter air held the warmth expelled by his lungs. The road looked plowed over where they were passing. It was taking less time than when Martin had driven them there.

His father was saying something about things eventually falling into place as an indication that they were right and proper. Johnny felt challenged but did not respond, because he felt like someone who would not live past the day.

Suddenly, like a stake driven into the ground, there stood Father Armand, with some men under the large tree in the clearing. Johnny parked where Martin had before. Upon seeing them, the men broke off to stand farther apart. Johnny and his father recognized the *barangay* captain but not the others, who held guns at their waists.

"Doctor," the *barangay* captain approached to open the car door. "Everything has been arranged. Your other son had cement delivered yesterday and we laid the foundation immediately. You'll like the spot I chose for the clinic, higher up than the one I pointed out to you."

Johnny and his father looked at each other in surprise. They had not planned on this, not so far ahead. "There must be some misunderstanding," his father said, getting out of the car.

"No, sir," the *barangay* captain said. "Not me. It's Father Armand who's confused. He's still insisting that the clinic is to be set up in his chapel...."

The men with guns at their sides laughed. "He must be crazy," the *barangay* captain continued, "but then anyone who would ordain himself has to be crazy. Perhaps you will explain to him, Doctor. He has been interfering with everything here. When I brought the message from Malacañang about the election, that priest who is not a priest told the people they should decide for themselves, that they should not surrender their registration cards because someone else would only vote in their place. Now that is subversion."

"My son and I decided to have the clinic set up temporarily in the chapel. Father Armand is right," the doctor explained, walking past the men toward the priest who was standing under the large tree, waiting.

"But the cement was sent to me. Your other son. And he promised," the *barangay* captain protested, "that his brother would take my son to the States." As the doctor went ahead to the priest, the official intercepted Johnny, "Your brother will be pleased. I dug it deeper than he ordered, because it had decomposed...but it's all done. I asked no questions and I don't want to know who it is; but we worked with proper respect and when the clinic is blessed, not by Father Armand, the body will rest in peace as surely as in any consecrated ground. I am a man of religion myself. I believe God wants me to use my authority here to suppress crime and subversion. Tell your brother that everything is all right.''

Johnny's imagination did not have far to leap to connect what the official said with Martin's plan to save Sylvia. He could hardly believe it! Pete Alvarez buried in the clinic's foundation the way relics of saints were imbedded beneath altars to consecrate them.

''I asked my friends to keep the others from prowling about, in case they saw or smelled something,'' the *barangay* captain said. ''That priest, for example, is always asking questions, minding everybody's business. He might have seen something.... He had the people all excited about the elections by saying that Malacañang should not distribute brown envelopes with money. It corrupts, he said. We should have dropped him in, too. Don't you want to see the foundation?''

The sun was now reflected in the fishponds, its light thrashing about on the surface like so many fish nibbling. The clarity of air mocked what the *barangay* captain had told Johnny, and he felt a pain rising to his ears, starting from between his shoulders. He did not want to be there, and in his mind he saw himself walking back to the car. However, he walked ahead to join his father and Father Armand, but with no words to repeat what he had been told.

Even more than on the day they first went there, the huts angled off like torn wings. The foul odor of garbage rose to all points of the compass.

''Let's go, Papá,'' he said, not taking the time to greet Father Armand, who was escorting his father into the chapel.

''Not yet,'' his father answered.

''Your patients can sit and wait under this tree,'' Father Armand was saying, when the *barangay* captain held him

166

by one shoulder and spun him around.

"That is all nonsense," the *barangay* captain said, surrounded by the men who looked more and more like convicts released for government service. "The clinic is where we laid down the foundation. Shall we go and inspect it, Doctor? Your other son chose the spot." As he waited, the *barangay* captain drove a stick into the ground between them, making tracks that a strange beast might stamp into the ground.

"I don't know what Martin told you," the doctor faced the official, "but Father Armand and I, yesterday...."

"Your son wanted to surprise you, Doctor. In fact, another day, and we would have had the roof and walls up." The *barangay* captain turned to Johnny as if they were accomplices in the matter.

"So you see, I was right," Father Armand stepped up to the *barangay* captain, a wide smile on his face. "This is where the Doctor wants his clinic."

The smile full of childlike trust was still on Father Armand's face when the men's guns fired. A different sound from Johnny's cry came back to him where he stood seeing Father Armand—the light gone from his eyes—fall slowly at the men's feet.

Blinded by the blood budding into dark and silent flowers on the ground, by the lights that lifted and pulled, Johnny remembered the nights he lay awake thinking of death.

As if the gunfire were the echo of their thoughts, people were soon running out of their huts directly to where Father Armand lay prostrate on the earth, in the gesture of an ordination. Carrying children in their arms and against their hips, or holding whatever they happened to be clutching, they stopped when they saw the body, their feet forming what could be the rim of some hidden well from which blood, not water, rose. "Father," some called out. Then, the silence of those afraid to look up from what they could

167

not bear to see.

Above them was a pale and ordinary sky.

After the shock had lifted, Johnny's father stepped toward the priest, but the *barangay* captain and the armed men stood in his way. "Don't touch him."

"Let my father," Johnny protested. Feeling nothing princely or even clear and true about himself, he also fell silent, standing once more as if nothing unprovoked, unholy, had taken place in his sight; nothing but another simple and arbitrary act that could not happen again in a million years, an isolated and unstable nucleus, perhaps, that had spent itself in fearsome excess.

And now, though nobody moved, the *barangay* captain stepped over Father Armand's body and spreading his legs, threw out a challenge to the others. "Anyone who wants the same, step out." When no one did, he added, "He thought he ran this place. You asked him to get water out of the ground, not just drinking water, but healing water. Well, go ask him now. Go ahead and ask him. See what he says."

The sun flamed like a burning candle. Wings heavily throbbing, flies began to hover over the split skull.

Johnny continued to stand there without feelings, though full of intimations that they had become a single flesh that sorrowed. From this he wanted absolution, wanted the camera to make the scene fade and pan to a different location, to zoom perhaps into a flower or make what was pressed against their faces blend with distance and disappear.

Transfixed as he was by the white cassock that appeared like water welling out of the ground, by children experiencing death without quite recognizing the evil, Johnny tried to summon some pious reflection to accompany his thoughts of Father Armand, an intensity to go with the dread that something had taken place to which his life should respond. But he could not act—and to say anything was to lie. He could only stand there like a bird with wings of stone attempting to fly.

The little boy rounding up the goats walked around those gathered about Father Armand's body. The crowd began to move, pushing Johnny out. Their footsteps left behind what appeared to be the imprint of the sun on the mud.

"Let's go," his father pulled Johnny away. "There's nothing we can do."

The wound was a large eye, tearing.

Johnny turned to go, thinking of the fireworks on the hill separating Belmont and Watertown each Fourth of July. The sun was lifting up from the trees that rimmed the fishponds, striking the crucifix inside the chapel. "Coming," Johnny answered.

Before he could reach his father, he saw trucks rolling towards them, preceded by a bulldozer. Dust rose heavily like smoke from ricefields being cleared of chaff. The squatters hurried towards their huts, to ransack them before they would be pulled away empty-handed. Children cried, begging to be snatched to safety.

A puppy ran between Johnny's legs. Tail tucked under its body, it went about in circles. A hen in the arms of a child lost its chicks under the tires of trucks that skidded into the earth, forming a barricade. Huts and earth were heaped together into rubble by the bulldozer. In that instant lost to reason, rags soaked in gasoline were lit, then thrown at the debris, which took instant light with the throbbing dance of lasers.

Johnny went weak at the sight of fires that shot up as if a new universe were exploding into place, a kind of celestial exhalation. He could not follow his father to the car. The flames seemed to come from deep within the earth, the heat from magma decomposing as it emerged, creating a burning crater.

Even the trees beyond the fires' reach seemed to suffer death.

Then with a suddenness too terrible to anticipate, the *barangay* captain and the armed men, their guns held out like the horns of beasts, began with their feet to roll Father Armand's body toward the blaze. As if a command had been given, at the same time the men bent down and, in one joint heave, tossed the body into the fire like a sin-offering. The air itself felt assaulted as flames embossed the body, burning away the soutane.

Johnny pgasped. As the fire sputtered and darker smoke rose, as the men straightened up, to Johnny their faces appeared as on the surface of still water to which a candle summoned the perpetrators of a crime.

Then, unable to use their guns on the soldiers to protect their own huts, the *barangay* captain and the men went running after the trucks, scrambling aboard with exultant cries that were also livid with pain.

For a moment Johnny could see what he was thinking, could hear his father saying over a cup of chocolate and *churros*, "I hoped you had come back to stay, though I knew it might not be. Here, anything is made right by law. We have lost our country...."

Meanwhile the fires spread beyond the dump, ran towards the trees and the edge of the fishponds. Having consumed what was left of huts and fences, partial doors and roofs, the uneven wheels of homemade carts, a cracked basin and mismatched wooden shoes, the fire burned on and on, feeding on the earth until the sun looked hanged above it.

Books from
Readers International

Sipho Sepamla, *A Ride on the Whirlwind*. This novel by one of South Africa's foremost black poets is set in the 1976 Soweto uprisings. "Not simply a tale of police versus rebels," said *World Literature Today*, "but a bold, sincere portrayal of the human predicament with which South Africa is faced." Hardback only, 244 pages. Retail price, US$12.50/£7.95 U.K.

Yang Jiang, *A Cadre School Life: Six Chapters*. Translated from the Chinese by Geremie Barmé and Bennett Lee. A lucid, personal meditation on the Cultural Revolution, the ordeal inflicted on 20 million Chinese, among them virtually all of the country's intellectuals. "Yang Jiang is a very distinguished old lady; she is a playwright; she translated Cervantes into Chinese...She lived through a disaster whose magnitude paralyzes the imagination...She is a subtle artist who knows how to say less to express more. Her *Six Chapters* are written with elegant simplicity." (Simon Leys, *The New Republic*) "An outstanding book, quite unlike anything else from 20th-century China...superbly translated." (*The Times Literary Supplement*). Hardback only, 91 pages. Retail price, $9.95/£6.50.

Sergio Ramírez, *To Bury Our Fathers*. Translated from Spanish by Nick Caistor. A panoramic novel of Nicaragua in the Somoza era, dramatically recreated by the country's leading prose artist. Cabaret singers, exiles, National Guardsmen, guerillas, itinerant traders, beauty queens, prostitutes and would-be presidents are the characters who people this sophisticated, lyrical and timeless epic of resistance and retribution. Paperback only, 253 pages. Retail price $8.95/£5.95.

Antonio Skármeta, *I Dreamt the Snow Was Burning*. Translated from Spanish by Malcolm Coad. A cynical country boy comes to Santiago to win at football and lose his virginity. The last days before the 1973 Chilean coup turn his world upside down. "With its vigour and fantasy, undoubtedly one of the best pieces of committed literature to emerge from Latin America," said *Le Monde*. 220 pages. Retail price, $14.95/£8.95 (hardback) $7.95/£4.95 (paperback).

Emile Habiby, *The Secret Life of Saeed, the Ill-Fated Pessoptimist*. Translated from the Arabic by Salma Khadra Jayyusi and Trevor Le Gassick. A comic epic of the Palestinian experience, the masterwork of a leading Palestinian journalist living in Israel. "...landed like a meteor

...in the midst of Arabic literature..." says Roger Hardy of *Middle East* magazine. Hardback only, 169 pages. Retail price, $14.95/£8.95.

Ivan Klíma, *My Merry Mornings*. Translated from Czech by George Theiner. Witty stories of the quiet corruption of Prague today. "Irrepressibly cheerful and successfully written" says the London *Financial Times*. Original illustrations for this edition by Czech artist Jan Brychta. Hardback, 154 pages. Retail price $14.95/£8.95.

Fire From the Ashes: Japanese stories on Hiroshima and Nagasaki, edited by Kenzaburo Oe. The first-ever collection in English of Stories by Japanese writers showing the deep effects of the A-bomb on their society over forty years. Hardback, 204 pages. Retail price $14.95/£8.95.

Linda Ty-Casper, *Awaiting Trespass: a Pasión*. Accomplished novel of Philippine society today. During a Passion Week full of risks and pilgrimages, the Gil family lives out the painful search of a nation for reason and nobility in irrational and ignoble times. 180 pages. Retail price $14.95/£8.95 (hardback), $7.95/£3.95 (paperback).

Janusz Anderman, *Poland Under Black Light*. Translated from Polish by Nina Taylor and Andrew Short. A talented young Polish writer, censored at home and coming into English for the first time, compels us into the eerie, Dickensian world of Warsaw under martial law. 150 pages. Retail price $12.50/£7.95 (hardback), $6.95/£3.95 (paperback).

Marta Traba, *Mothers and Shadows*. Translated from Spanish by Jo Labanyi. Out of the decade just past of dictatorship, torture and disappearances in the Southern Cone of Latin America comes this fascinating encounter between women of two different generations which evokes the tragedy and drama of Argentina, Uruguay and Chile. "Fierce, intelligent, moving" says *El Tiempo* of Bogotá. 200 pages. Retail price $14.95/£8.95 (hardback), $7.95/£3.95 (paperback).

Osvaldo Soriano, *A Funny, Dirty Little War*. Translated from Spanish by Nick Caistor. An important novel that could only be published in Argentina after the end of military rule, but which has now received both popular and critical acclaim — this black farce relives the beginnings of the Peronist "war against terrorism" as a bizarre and bloody comic romp. 150 pages. Retail price $12.50/£7.95 (hardback), $6.95/£3.95 (paperback).

READERS INTERNATIONAL publishes contemporary literature of quality from Latin America and the Caribbean, the Middle East, Asia, Africa and Eastern Europe. Many of these books were initially banned at home: READERS INTERNATIONAL is particularly committed to conserving literature in danger. Each book is current — from the past 10 years. And each is new to readers here. READERS INTERNATIONAL is registered as a not-for-profit, tax-exempt organisation in the United States of America.

If you wish to know more about Readers International's series of contemporary world literature, please write to 503 Broadway, 5th Floor, New York, NY 10012, USA; or to the Editorial Branch, 8 Strathray Gardens, London NW3 4NY, England. Orders in North America can be placed directly with Readers International, Subscription/Order Department P.O. Box 959, Columbia, Louisiana 71418, USA.